A strong wind came
up at Longarm's back...

He had to brace himself against the rock. Then he took a careful step backward away from the edge of the quarried cliff. One misstep here, and a man would fall to certain death on the hard red stone far below.

He pulled a cheroot from his pocket, bit off the twisted tobacco at the tip, and spat it out. As he pulled out a match, he dropped the damn cheroot onto the stony, nearly bare soil at the lip of the cliff.

As he bent to pick up the cigar, he heard the angry, quick sizzle of a large-caliber slug passing overhead ...just where his head had been a moment before.

By the time he heard the hollow, distinctive report of a muzzle blast from a heavy rifle, Custis Long was already sprawled face down on the ground with his Colt in his hand, but with no damned idea of where his target might be...

--*- TABOR EVANS -*--

LONGARM

AND THE
COWBOY'S REVENGE

A JOVE BOOK

LONGARM AND THE COWBOY'S REVENGE

A Jove Book/published by arrangement with
the author

PRINTING HISTORY
Jove edition/July 1985

ISBN: 0-515-08232-5

Jove books are published by The Berkley Publishing Group,
200 Madison Avenue, New York, N.Y. 10016. The words
"A JOVE BOOK" and the "J" with sunburst are trademarks
belonging to Jove Publications, Inc.

PRINTED IN THE UNITED STATES OF AMERICA

LONGARM

AND THE COWBOY'S REVENGE

Chapter 1

Longarm stomped his way into United States Marshal Billy Vail's private office, the anger in him so strong he could taste it, the biting, nasty flavor of bile on his tongue so acute that even the flavor of an expensive after-dinner cigar could not soothe it. The marshal's best deputy did not remove his hat or bother to give his superior any of the customary greetings, not even a friendly insult. He stood with his boots planted firmly on the unpolished hardwood of the government office flooring, hands—fists really—planted just as firmly against his lean hips, and glared down at the balding, pink-cheeked man who was in charge of the Justice Department's efforts to maintain law and order in the Denver district.

"All right, damn it," Deputy Marshal Custis Long declared without preamble. "What's all this bullshit?"

Vail looked up at him from the swivel chair behind

his desk with no apparent signs of reaction except a gentle half-smile and a blink or two.

"You promised me, damn it," Long went on angrily. "You promised. It's the Fourth of fucking July weekend coming up, and I got some free time coming. You *know* that, Billy, and I got plans made. For the whole weekend. And now your damned messenger comes an' tells me I'm supposed to report here for a job, an' then he runs off into the night like he's scared. Well, he ought to be. If you think for one minute that—"

"Shut up, Custis," the marshal said. His tone was mild enough, but it held a cutting edge of authority that penetrated even Longarm's distress.

"But..."

"Deputy. Hush your mouth and listen to me before you bite." Vail paused and smiled. "Anger is bad for the digestion, you know. If you don't calm down soon you're going to have heartburn." The marshal waited patiently for his words to take effect, looking up at the tall, lean deputy with his deep tan and sweeping brown moustache. "Sit," he said, pointing to a carved wood chair with red leather upholstery and brass tacks.

"But..."

"Sit."

Longarm sat. He was still upset, but perhaps a little less so.

"Now," Billy Vail said, "isn't that more comfortable?" He smiled. "Have a nice dinner, did you?"

"What the—"

"Send a nice wire to the pretty nurse confirming the weekend plans?"

"How the hell do you know about her?"

Vail's smile did not change, which Longarm found

2

all the more annoying. Somehow, without having to leave this office, even at eight o'clock at night, Billy Vail always seemed to know what every one of his men was up to, in their personal as well as official lives.

"I suppose you know the young lady's name too," Longarm challenged, intending to find some small measure of flaw in the marshal's information. The lady's name was something Longarm had not mentioned to anyone in Denver.

Vail grinned. He quite obviously knew that he was being tested. "Morrison? No, Morrisey. Miss Ruth Morrisey. Sanatorium nurse from Manitou, if I remember correctly." The grin got wider. Billy Vail leaned back in his chair and folded his hands across a stomach that was becoming somewhat more ample than had been the case when he was a field man himself.

"Shit," Longarm muttered. He really did not know how the man did it.

"Can we quit playing games now, Custis? Are you ready to listen to me?"

Longarm grunted something that might have been acquiescence. He took a last drag on the excellent cigar, much better leaf than the cheroots he usually smoked, and leaned forward to stub it out in the ashtray on Billy Vail's desk.

"Good," the marshal said. "Now then, Longarm —" His use of the deputy's nickname indicated that his mood was good now. "—I have not forgotten that I promised you the weekend. Not at all."

Longarm grunted. He did not say anything, but he did feel somewhat better about the after-hours summons to Vail's office. The weekend trip with Ruth

3

had been a long time in the planning, and it would be their first opportunity to spend any real amount of time together. Thus far the pressures of either his job or hers had kept their infrequent meetings entirely too innocent.

"I called you in tonight, Longarm, so you can take care of this one tiny thing before the weekend. It won't interfere at all."

"You say that, but every damn time—"

Vail held a hand up to stop the impending flood of complaint. "I know. Assignments tend to take their own courses, regardless of what we plan. This is different."

Longarm grunted again.

"No assignment this time, Deputy. Just a simple visit to a man in prison. I called you in tonight so you can be on the morning train south. You have more than enough time to go down to the prison and talk to this bird, then be back here in plenty of time for your holiday. As a matter of fact," Vail suggested, "the train passes within a few miles of Manitou. I would have no objection to a layover there on your way back to Denver."

Longarm looked at his boss with suspicion. This sort of thing was not exactly what he would have expected from Marshal William Vail. "There's a clinker in this someplace," he said.

"Not at all."

Longarm withheld judgment on that for the moment. "Go on."

"It is quite simple, really. Do you remember a man named Alfred Sweeley?"

"Alfred . . ." Longarm's first reaction was denial, then he made the connection. "You mean Pop Swee-

4

ley. Is that old son of a bitch still alive? Lordy, he was one of the first arrests I made when I came with the outfit; it's been that long ago." Longarm shook his head. "I still think the old bastard should've been strung up along with his pals."

"The State of Colorado, in its infinite wisdom," Vail smiled again, "saw the matter differently. State jurisdiction and all that. Besides, if Sweeley paroles out on the life sentence he's serving now, he still faces federal charges."

"I still think that's one of the meanest men I've met in my life, Billy," Longarm said.

He was remembering the case now, although it had been years since he had thought about Pop Sweeley and his gang. Sweeley had been a member of a gang of cutthroats who operated in the mining camps of Georgetown and Central City and Idaho Springs. Longarm still maintained that the old fossil was also the gang's leader, but he had never been able to prove that.

Their specialty had been to use a network of willing whores to spot miners who were carrying heavy pokes. The girl would lure a man into a darkened room, and then the gang would slip out when the poor bastard was in the midst of action and knife him. Shot out of the saddle, so to speak. The gang's trademark had come to be a wardrobe in a whore's crib, a place where the waiting knifeman could hide. It was that unusual touch in the suspect cribs that had finally given them away during the investigation.

What made Longarm regard them all as being so brutal was the fact that in no instance did any victim of Pop Sweeley's gang survive the robbery.

Any halfway reasonable robber would have been

content with bopping his victim on the back of the head and taking his pouch. But Sweeley, possibly to protect his string of whores from exposure—and himself from their confessions if they were exposed—always made sure that his victims were cold beef before he dumped them into a convenient mineshaft. There was no way anyone would ever know how many victims there had actually been. The ones whose bodies were recovered had all died from a single deft slice into the side of the neck which severed the jugular vein and resulted in a swift, somewhat messy death.

It must have been a real bother having to clean up after each of the killings, Longarm thought. But then, the gang probably made the whores do that part of the work.

"Old bastard," Longarm muttered.

Pop Sweeley had been the only gang member Longarm had been able to positively identify and place under arrest at the time. He should have hanged, Longarm still believed, and would have, except that he was able to save his own neck by ratting on his fellow gang members. The bargain had been a simple one. Sweeley would identify the others if he were assured of no worse than a life sentence in prison. So, in the long run, Pop Sweeley formally testified against his pals, and they all hanged while the old buzzard went happily off to a life in the stone cells at Canon City.

At that time, still new to the workaday world of real-life law enforcement, Longarm had considered the whole thing to be a miscarriage of justice. He still did.

"So why should I be remembering Pop Sweeley

6

after all this time?" Longarm asked.

"He wants you to come visit him," Billy Vail said blandly.

Chapter 2

Longarm could scarcely believe he was having to go all the way to Canon City in the Arkansas Valley just to meet the whim of a convicted murderer in the stone-walled lifers' cells. But that was where he now found himself, jolting and jouncing along in a Denver and Rio Grande smoker car.

And, to top it off, he did not even know *why* he was going. Aside, that is, from the pointedly obvious fact that Marshal Billy Vail had ordered him to go.

No one, including Vail, seemed to know why Pop Sweeley was insisting now that he get to see and talk to the man who had put him behind bars all those years before.

The only thing Billy had been able to say for sure was that Sweeley was demanding to talk to Deputy Marshal Custis Long and no one else. He had information of great but unspecified importance to relate, the old codger kept insisting to the prison officials.

As far as Deputy Marshal Long was concerned, the whole thing could have been handled more simply if only Billy Vail, or one of those prison officials before him, had had the good and common sense to tell the old bastard to shut his mouth and serve out his time in silence. That way Longarm could have gotten an early start on the holiday weekend without the nuisance of this trip.

On the other hand, there still was the possibility, even the likelihood, of a layover at Manitou before the official start of the work-free weekend. That was something, anyway.

Longarm sighed and stared at the rolling, already browning grasslands to the east of the steel rails. On the other side of the coach would be the harsh, rugged rise of the Front Range mountains, crowned even at this time of year by expanses of snow atop Pikes Peak.

Like it or not, Vail had insisted that the trip be made, that the conversation Sweeley was demanding take place.

The marshal had hinted—but carefully not said outright—that pressure was being applied to insure that the meeting take place as quickly as possible even though virtually all the government offices in Denver were already slowing their workloads in anticipation of the long, festive weekend. The Fourth fell on a Monday this year, giving the governmental employees a three-day weekend, and that rarity seemed to add flavor to the anticipation of the speeches and the flag-waving and the fireworks to come.

The normal inclination, Longarm knew, would have been for this meeting to take place, if it absolutely had to take place, next week. After all, where the hell was Sweeley going to go in the meantime? The old man would still be there whenever Longarm found it convenient to see him.

But Billy Vail had hinted that someone outside the Justice Department was interested in having the talk take place as quickly as possible. And any pressure of that nature was most assuredly political.

Who and why Longarm could not imagine. But that was the only way he could figure it.

Whatever was going on here, he hoped it was not going to turn out to be something that would interfere with the plans he and Ruth had made. If that happened he was going to be *really* mad.

Still, a man never knows. And an emergency message could all too easily catch up with him at any time.

Long experience with that sort of thing had led Longarm to carry more with him for the short journey than the simple overnight bag that would otherwise have been justified. Back in the baggage car he had his carpetbag complete with all his normal traveling gear plus his McClellan saddle and scabbarded Winchester even though he should, as far as he or anyone else might know, have absolutely no need to fork a horse between now and his return to Denver.

As always, of course, he also wore his double-action Colt Thunderer revolver and, tucked away in a vest pocket at the end of his watch chain, a brass .41-caliber derringer. Those he would no more leave at home than a lady would walk away without her handbag or a bank clerk forget his spectacles. The weapons were as much a part of his everyday dress as were his Stetson hat, tweed coat, and calf-high boots.

Longarm sighed again and pulled a cheroot from his coat pocket. He nipped the end off and spat it in the general direction of a cuspidor on the floor of the rail coach, pulled a match from another pocket and flicked it alight. He would have liked a drink of Maryland rye to cut through the coal dust and acrid smoke that drifted in through the open coach window, but the nearest bottle he knew of was back in the baggage car with the rest of his things. Pity, he thought. One of these days he was going to have to invest in a silver flask for occasions such as this.

Since there was nothing better to do while he rode, he settled for admiring the neck and profile of a nicely dressed woman riding ahead of him in the coach.

She was a pretty enough thing, with pale red hair and a slim but attractive figure. Certainly pretty enough to ease the boredom of travel.

He found it rather a shame that she was not alone. But then, had she been alone, she most certainly would not have been riding in the smoker.

She was traveling with a man who was dressed well enough. The quality of cloth in his suit and the cut of the tailor's work looked expensive.

But there was something about the fellow that made Longarm wonder both about the recentness of his wealth and the tastes of his undeniably attractive companion.

Longarm thought the man looked uncomfortable in the clothing, as if he would have been more at home in a flannel shirt and denim trousers. Probably a prospector or hardrock man new to his money, Longarm thought idly. And not worth worrying about. Longarm gave the man the briefest of inspections and then spent the rest of the time down to Pueblo cov-

11

ertly admiring the young lady. She was much more interesting to watch.

At Pueblo he left the train and gathered his gear for the switch off the main line to the narrow-gauge run along the Arkansas to Canon City. The tracks went somewhat farther, having already reached Buena Vista this year in the rush to reach Leadville and the rich freight contracts that would belong to the first of several railroads now building toward that current queen city of the mountain mining camps.

At least the westbound section of D&RG track could be picked up from the same terminal, avoiding the nuisance of having luggage hauled across the sleepy town just to make the next train connection, as was so often necessary when passing through Denver.

Longarm gathered his things and carried them with him, not entirely trusting them to the mercies of baggage handlers, while he had pie and coffee in one of the greasy spoon cafes adjacent to the depot.

When his Ingersoll told him that it was nearly time for the posted departure of the westbound passenger, he paid for the snack and went back to the platform.

The nice-looking redhead and her hulking companion were waiting there for the same connection west. The man was much taller and heavier than Longarm had thought before.

Going home, Longarm suspected, or going back for a try at a second fortune.

This time the unmatched couple boarded a regular coach while Longarm once again sought out the additional room and comfort of the smoker car. He did not see them again and certainly did not think any more about the redhead once she was out of sight. He was, after all, not the sort of man who will poach on another's preserves.

It was late afternoon, getting on toward evening, before Longarm finally left the train at Canon City. From the steps of the railroad depot he could see the walls and watchtowers of the Colorado State Prison a half mile or less to the west.

Even from there the gray rock looked cold and uncompromising. Between that and the arid, often suffocatingly hot climate of Canon City, the prison was not a place for a man to aspire to.

The citizens of the town—which, in spite of its primary reason for existence, was charming and modern—could enjoy the shade of the many trees planted beside the streets and avenues of their community. They could stroll in the green parks or along the swirling whitewater river. But the prisoners behind those high, forbidding walls could only suffer in their confinement. Longarm had been here often enough in the past to know the prison better than he would ever have chosen to do, and he felt no envy for the criminals who were confined here.

He stood on the depot steps and consulted his pocket watch. It was late, but not so late that he could not expect to see Sweeley tonight if he so insisted.

On the other hand, he was hungry and tired after a full day on the trains. The eastbound that he would have to take tomorrow to make his connection back to Denver would not be leaving until early afternoon. He could as easily have his talk with Sweeley in the morning, take a leisurely lunch, and still have more than enough time to board the eastbound train for Pueblo.

13

Decided, he thought. He snapped shut the case of the Ingersoll and tucked it back into his vest pocket, picked up his carpetbag and saddle, and began the two-block walk to the Hotel Gerrard, where he had stayed before. A tub of hot water was supplied free with each room at the Gerrard, and government vouchers were as welcome there as cash. Both were advantages, to Longarm's thinking, particularly the appeal of a bath after a full day of being pelted with cinders from those damnable smokestacks on the trains.

And, as he also remembered very, very well from past trips down this way, the bartender at the Gerrard kept a stock of excellent Maryland rye.

Chapter 3

Longarm finished tying his string tie and slicked his hair back with a matched pair of military brushes that had been given to him by a lady. That had been several months ago, and he was not sure yet if he liked them or not, but the gift had been thoughtful. He dropped them back into his carpetbag. He felt better now, freshly bathed and in a clean shirt. He tugged his vest back in place after dislodging it with the upraised arm motions and checked to make sure the Colt was riding where it ought to, to the left of his belt buckle, positioned carefully for a cross-body draw. Not that he expected to need it, not this trip, but it never paid to be careless. He plucked a cheroot from the handful that lay on the hotel-room dresser and lighted it. All he needed now was the return of his coat and he could go out for a drink and a meal. Normally he would have brushed the coat clean himself, but the cinders and soot left in the fabric after a day-long train ride tended to smear if the cleaning were not done carefully. He had treated himself to a professional effort this time.

He had time to finish the smoke and enjoy several pulls from the bottle he generally carried in his bag before he finally heard footsteps in the hallway. The steps stopped outside his closed door. A moment later there was a soft tapping on the wooden door.

"Yes?"

"Your cleaning, sir."

It sounded like the girl who had been sent to pick up the coat and take it away for cleaning. Even so, Longarm was standing to the side of the doorframe when he unlocked the door and let it swing open.

There was only the girl in the hallway. She was smiling and holding his coat, pressed as well as cleaned and carried back to him on a wooden hanger.

"Thanks." He took the coat from her and let her help him into it. He paid her and added a small tip, which earned him a bright, cheerful smile.

"Thank *you*, sir."

He winked at her. She was a cute kid, fourteen or maybe fifteen, with dimpled cheeks and a pleasant demeanor. He wondered if her family ran the local laundry and cleaners, or if she was already having to help earn her way in the world.

The girl went off down the hallway with the now empty coat hanger in one hand and the coins in the other. Longarm paused only long enough to lock the hotel-room door behind him and then followed her.

He trailed her downstairs and across the small lobby. The bar at the Gerrard was excellent but the food only so-so. Hungrier now than he was thirsty after the several nips he had had out of his own bottle, Longarm continued on through the lobby and out into the cooling early evening. The afternoon heat had been extreme, but now that the sun had disappeared behind the mountains to the west the air felt refreshing and clean.

The girl turned to the right when she left the hotel. She obviously knew where she was going. Longarm paused on the narrow porch for a moment, refreshing his memory of the town and taking a look at the signs hung out along the main street. Then he too turned to the right and walked toward a cafe he could see in the next block. He had not eaten there before, but the sign outside the place was freshly painted and neatly lettered. Maybe that meant something about the quality of food he could expect inside. He hoped so.

Longarm descended the steps from the Gerrard's porch onto the sidewalk about the time the girl from the laundry reached the alley at the end of the Gerrard building.

He saw her stop there and look apprehensively to her right, into the mouth of the alley.

A man stepped briefly into sight, took her arm, and pulled her into the alley with him. Longarm's pace quickened.

The girl was crying. She was young enough—and frightened enough—that she cried like a child, not like a young woman. Without dignity or thought of her appearance. Her eyes streamed and her nose ran. Spots of color brighter than any artificial cosmetic blotched her cheeks, and her shoulders shook with the racking efforts of her sobs.

"D-d-don't, Larry. Please, d-don't."

The young man she was facing laughed at her distress. He was probably not more than eighteen or nineteen, but he was heavily built and was in need of a shave.

"Gimme," he said.

"I gotta take this money back to Ma, Larry. You know I do. Please."

"Gimme here, Matty. Right now, or I'll go tell your ma what you and Bubby was doing in Mr. Simpson's carriage house." He grinned at her and held his hand out.

The girl cried all the harder. With the hand that still clung to the empty coat hanger, she noisily wiped her nose, but she extended her other clenched fist out to Larry.

"That's better, Matty," he said.

"Or possibly not," another voice interjected.

Both heads turned, the boy's and the girl's. The fading evening light was not good enough for Larry to get a good look at the man who was leaning casually against the hotel wall, but Matty recognized him as the tall and rather excitingly handsome man she had just delivered the coat to upstairs. She remembered that he had the clearest, brownest eyes she had ever seen. That was not all she remembered about him either. It had been difficult for her to look at him and then accept that tip and friendly wink from him without blushing. Now she did blush. She hoped he had not heard that awful thing Larry had said about her and Bubby. Especially since it was not true. Well, not *entirely* true, anyway.

Larry glared and hunched his shoulders, but he did not seem to know what to do about the presence of the tall stranger.

"You know, Larry," the brown-eyed man said in a soft drawl, "taking candy from babies would be even easier." He smiled. "About your style too, I'd say."

"You better get out of here, mister," Larry blustered. "This ain't your nevermind."

The man laughed. "I've been standing here wondering just what I ought to do about you, Larry. Now I think I've figured it out."

Matty stood in shocked and wide-eyed amazement while the tall man walked forward just as casually as if he was walking up to the counter at the hotel lobby to ask for a room. No more sign of hurry or trouble than that at all.

"What I think you need," the tall man said, "is a spanking."

No one had ever spanked Larry Frye. Not even back when Larry used to go to school. Mr. Porter had tried once, but Larry and his brothers got together and beat up on Mr. Porter. Mr. Porter quit teaching after that, and the Frye brothers, all three of them, got thrown out of school. But no one had ever spanked *any* of them.

Now this man said he was going to spank Larry. Matty wanted to warn him not to. She really did. But by then it was too late.

Larry's face sulled up and got red the way it always did when he got mad about something, and then he stepped forward and took a punch at the tall man.

Larry was a lot younger, of course, but he was almost as tall as the brown-eyed man and was built much heavier. Matty was half sure that Larry would be able to beat up the tall man just like he and his brothers had done to poor Mr. Porter.

But Larry threw that one punch, and then the tall

19

man moved so fast that Matty couldn't hardly see what all was happening. It was just that quick.

Larry punched at him and then the tall man just seemed to *flow* from one place to another, and then he was behind Larry and Larry was all bent over and the tall man was holding Larry's wrist with Larry's arm levered up behind his back. Matty knew how bad that could hurt. Her brothers had done it to her often enough when they were scrapping. Ma let them get away with that a little when she baited them into a tussle, even though they weren't ever allowed to hit her or they'd really have got it. But an arm held up like that could really *hurt*.

Larry must have been hurting. He squawled and tried to kick once, then yelped even louder and held still when the tall man pushed up a little further on that arm.

Matty could scarcely believe any of this. The brown-eyed man wasn't even breathing hard and didn't look even *mad* or anything. He still looked and acted as casual as a grown-up lighting a pipe.

The tall man jammed Larry's nose up against the wood siding on Jamison's bakery, reached around to unbuckle Larry's belt, and then—Matty gasped—used Larry's own belt to whip him with.

He laid onto him hard too. The sound of the leather smacking into Larry's bottom was sharp and loud. Matty knew she probably should have blushed, but she did not.

Larry hollered and wiggled, but he wasn't going anywhere. Not with the man holding him like that while he gave the licking.

Matty thought this was probably the most exciting, *unbelievable* thing she had ever witnessed.

And Larry was *crying*. Now Larry Frye was actually crying. She could hear him. He was bawling worse than any of her brothers ever used to, even back when they were little kids.

No one would ever believe this. If she ever got up the nerve to tell anyone and risk Larry finding out that she had told, no one, absolutely *no* one, would ever believe that she had seen Larry Frye cry.

That thought jarred her.

Larry wasn't thinking about her right now, but he sure would later on. Especially if he knew she'd seen all of this.

She knew she really ought to stay and warn the handsome, brown-eyed man about Larry and his older brothers.

But if Larry knew that she'd seen all this she would *never* be safe again.

Matty Armister turned and gathered up her skirts, her money and her very own tip still clutched in one hand, and ran like hell for the other end of the alley.

When she got home, breathing hard and more than half scared, she did not tell anyone what she had seen and heard. It was hard not to tell. But then no one would have believed her anyway.

Chapter 4

Longarm prodded a piece of cold potato that was nested in the congealing grease left from his steak, decided he would rather have the flavor of red meat be the last taste in his mouth from the good meal, and pushed his plate away. A final cup of coffee now, or the short trip back to the Gerrard for a shot of rye? It was not the sort of decision he minded having to make.

The decision was made for him when a handsome blonde woman stopped beside his table. He looked at her while he went through the polite motions of rising to greet her.

She was still quite attractive, but laugh lines radiated from the corners of her mouth and a lacework of wrinkles was beginning to show around her eyes, quite fetchingly clear and blue, and on her neck. Her hands were rough and reddened by hard work. She was dressed neatly but not well. Middle to late thirties, he thought, and not a member of the upper crust.

"Sir?"

"Ma'am?" Still standing, he refolded his napkin and laid it beside his plate. He was sure he had never met her before. He was sure he would have remembered if he had. She was attractive but, more than that, she looked like the kind of woman who would be a pleasure for her company alone.

"You look," she said, "excuse me for interrupting your dinner, but you look like the gentleman Matty described."

Longarm smiled. That explained it. "No interruption, ma'am. I was already finished. And you would be Matty's mother?"

"Yes."

Longarm introduced himself by name but not by title. It often bothered people to talk with an officer of the law, and the distinction did not seem necessary here.

"Patricia Armister," the woman said. She extended her hand for Longarm to touch briefly in acknowledgement of the introduction. "I would have come sooner to thank you for helping my daughter, Mr. Long, but it took me some time to get Matty to tell me why she was bothered this evening."

Longarm smiled again. "I'm sorry if she was flustered, but she had every reason to be. Your daughter seems like a sweet little girl. No reason for her to have to put up with bullying."

"Well, I do want to thank you, Mr. Long. But..." Mrs. Armister seemed worried too.

Longarm remembered his manners and motioned the woman to a chair across the table. There was no need for them to stand if they were going to continue talking, which she obviously wanted to do. "Join me for dessert, ma'am? I would appreciate the company. If it would not compromise you, that is." The cafe was not full, but there were others in the room. Mr. Armister might be the jealous type, or Canon City might be the talkative kind.

Mrs. Armister smiled briefly. "Widows without position are not susceptible to compromise, Mr. Long." She accepted his invitation and waited quite naturally for him to assist her with the chair.

A widow, eh? Longarm thought. Not that he intended to take any advantages, but the thought was interesting. He returned to his own chair, and the waiter appeared a moment later with a cup of tea for Mrs. Armister—obviously she was no stranger here—and a refill for Longarm's coffee cup. He ordered dessert for both of them. The choices were dried-apple pie or dried-apple pie.

"You were about to say something, Mrs. Armister?" he suggested when the waiter had gone to get their dried-apple pie.

"Yes. I . . . I wanted to tell you how much I appreciate your helping Matty. Of course. But . . . oh, I don't know how to put this, exactly."

"It was something anyone would have been willing to do for the child," Longarm said.

Mrs. Armister looked troubled. "Not around here, Mr. Long. And that, you see, is the problem."

"Oh?"

"Larry . . . that's the boy you spanked this evening, and wouldn't I or half the rest of the town have been happy to see *that* . . . he and his brothers are what you might call the rowdy element here."

Longarm smiled. If that dim-witted young lout was

the rowdy element of the community, Canon City must be a very nice place indeed, he thought. In a deputy United States marshal's line of work—and in most of the places that work took him—Larry would hardly be considered worth noticing.

"You seem not to be taking me seriously, Mr. Long."

"It isn't that, ma'am. I was just thinking about something else."

"Please. The reason I came here, beyond thanking you, of course, was to warn you. Larry is the youngest of three brothers. They are very close, and they can be quite mean. The older boys baby Larry something awful. They are too protective of him, really, but no one here is quite up to stopping them." Her eyes widened. "The older boys carry guns, Mr. Long."

Longarm smiled again. "I have one of those myself, ma'am. But I do thank you for your concern."

"Really. They can be quite dangerous."

"Then I shall have to be quite careful."

The dried-apple pie was delivered, and Longarm changed the subject adroitly.

While they ate, Longarm learned that Mrs. Armister had been widowed for three years. Her husband had been a guard at the prison since the territorial days. The woman did not say so, but Longarm got the impression the late Mr. Armister had been a supervisor of some sort there. He died in an escape attempt by a number of the harder prisoners.

"Did he stop them?" Longarm asked.

"Yes, he did."

Longarm nodded and took a forkful of the pie.

"He was quite proud of that. I . . . we all are grateful that he lived long enough afterward to know that he succeeded. He was a very proud man."

Longarm nodded again. "How many children do you have?"

She smiled. "Two boys and Matty. Matty is my middle child." She sighed. "They are growing up so fast now. Before long I shall have to start calling Matty Matilda."

She talked on. The children had all been born in Colorado Territory except their oldest, who had been born back home in Virginia.

Longarm wondered about Mrs. Armister's family background. Her speech and table manners were those of someone much higher than a prison-town laundress, but she made neither statement nor intimation that could have been taken as complaint or as brag. He liked that about her.

The War Between the States was some years past now, but it had left a great many lingering scars, left a great many fine families in permanently altered condition. And Virginia had been one of those areas hurt the most severely. Longarm was careful to avoid mention of his own West Virginia background. That was a subject that still rankled with many Virginians.

Not that he was ashamed of his home country. Far from it. He only wanted to avoid giving offense.

When the pie was gone, Longarm paid the bill and helped Mrs. Armister with her chair. "May I see you home, ma'am?"

"That won't be necessary, Mr. Long."

"I mean you no harm, Mrs. Armister. It's only that I'll feel better knowing you are all right. After all, you did come out this evening on my behalf. The least I can do is see you safely home now."

She smiled. "My refusal was a matter of your convenience, sir, not my own safety. You give the impres-

26

sion of being a gentleman." She hesitated and gave him a frank and open inspection. "At least where ladies are concerned. Perhaps my warning was unnecessary after all."

Longarm was not entirely sure how he should take that. But he was beginning to believe that Mrs. Patricia Armister was an intelligent and perceptive woman, regardless of her current occupation.

"I would be pleased if you were to see me home, Mr. Long," she said.

She led the way from the cafe and turned to her right, toward the far edge of the small town.

Without thinking about it, Longarm found himself offering Mrs. Armister his elbow in the approved protocol for strolling on a summer's evening.

And, just as naturally, she placed her fingertips lightly on his arm in the accepted response.

Her hand was not gloved, but he thought it should have been. For just a scant, flickering moment there, she made a curious gesture with her free hand and then dropped the hand with what might have been a slight blush, although the light was too poor for him to be sure of that.

He thought he should have recognized the stillborn gesture, but at first it would not come to him. Then it did. It was the motion she would have made had she been raising a parasol to twirl against her shoulder. Longarm pretended not to have noticed.

Chapter 5

"That's him, Lonnie. That's *him* with the damn brat's ma."

Longarm recognized the voice. It was Larry Frye. The hulking youngster and two even larger companions—the much feared brothers, Longarm assumed—stepped out of the shadows of a cottonwood tree near Mrs. Armister's tiny but very well-cared-for house.

Longarm smiled at them. To himself he was thinking: *Larry and now Lonnie; probably the third one is named Louie. With names like that they should join a traveling tent troupe and go on the road. Maybe the kid would make a better comedian than thug.*

"This is convenient," Longarm said easily. "I was going to look you boys up, anyway." He grinned at them. "Wanted to have a word with you about leaving folks alone. Particularly folks by the name of Armister."

"Bastard," one of the older brothers spat.

"Keep that up, son, and I'll also have to teach you some manners. It ain't polite to cuss in front of a lady."

"Bastard," the other older brother said. "You beat up on my little brother. An' we're gonna give you a stomping you won't never get over."

Longarm managed a look of innocence, an unstraying lamb falsely accused. "Me? Why, boys, I never beat up on your little brother. I spanked him is what I done. And high time somebody did, too, let me tell you." The three Fryes started forward, although Longarm noticed that Larry was lagging somewhat behind his older and larger relations.

"Which one of you is Louie?" he asked.

The Fryes, puzzled, halted their supposed-to-be-menacing stalk for a moment.

"I am," the one on the right said.

They probably did not understand at all when Longarm burst into laughter at the accuracy of his own guessing.

"Just a minute then, boys," Longarm said. "No need for Mrs. Armister to see any of this."

Completely ignoring the Frye brothers, Longarm turned to the lady on his arm. "I think you should go inside now, ma'am. Are the children safe?"

She nodded. She looked nervous. "I . . . sent them to stay with friends for the night. I was afraid something like this might happen."

Longarm gave her an easy smile. "But, ma'am, nothing has happened. No harm will come to you or to your children."

Her fingers tightened on his arm. "The way you say that, sir, I almost believe you."

29

"My word on it, ma'am," Longarm said gallantly.

Still ignoring the blustering but confused Frye boys, Longarm led the woman to the front door of her home and removed his Stetson to her as he opened the door to see her safely inside. "Good night, Mrs. Armister." He paused and added, "Meeting you has been an unexpected pleasure."

She looked at him for a moment, giving him a look that seemed to combine current speculation with a distant memory. Then she smiled and extended one hand toward him while with the other she gathered her skirts and dropped into a curtsy.

Longarm touched her fingertips with his own and bowed low over the offered hand in a motion that almost, but not quite, brought his lips into contact with the back of her hand. "Ma'am."

Mrs. Armister stepped back into her crudely built little house and closed the rough-hewn plank door. The setting was wrong, Longarm thought, but the feeling was entirely correct. Meeting the lady from Virginia somehow made him feel better about himself. It made the trip down here to Canon City quite worthwhile, regardless of what Pop Sweeley might have to say tomorrow.

He turned back to the definitely bewildered Frye brothers and gave them a bright, cheerful smile. "Come along boys. We can discuss this better elsewhere."

Lonnie and dumb Larry seemed buffaloed enough to go along with it, but Louie was recovering from the odd spectacle he had seen but not understood.

"Damn it, mister, we come here to stomp the shit outa you, not go on some fuckin' promenade with you."

Longarm's eyes narrowed, and for the first time

the easy good humor left his face. Now that Mrs. Armister was no longer in immediate danger, the Frye brothers were able, if they bothered to look, to see the steel that lay beneath the surface.

"I won't tell you again, boy. You don't use that kind of language where a lady might hear." The walls of the house were not so thick that they would block the sound of voices, and Longarm genuinely did not want Patricia Armister to have to hear.

"You're makin' me mad, mister. Keep it up an' me an' my brothers won't just stomp you, we'll leave you layin' dead."

Longarm walked toward him. All three brothers began to back away. In spite of their bluster, they were beginning to look a bit nervous now.

The sensible thing to do, Longarm thought, would probably be to drag iron and take all three of them to jail. He could book them on charges of threatening the life of a peace officer. That was a crime on the books here, albeit a rarely enforced one.

But a picayune charge like that would give them probably no more than a week in jail. A month in the local pokey at the very worst. And when they got out, Longarm would be long gone and Mrs. Amister and her children would still be here, still vulnerable to their anger.

He wanted to make more of an impression on them than that.

He left the Colt untouched in its holster and continued walking toward them while all three of the bullies back-pedaled slowly away. Longarm reached into a hip pocket for his riding gloves and pulled them on. There seemed no point in damaging his hands while he taught these young idiots a lesson.

He reached the nearest of them and without breaking stride snapped a hard, straight right onto the point of Louie's jaw. His timing was carefully calculated to put the full weight of his body behind the punch. It knocked Louie off his feet and sent the other two into a bellowing rage.

For a few moments there the night seemed full of fists and elbows.

As Longarm had more than half expected, the Fryes knew nothing about fighting, only about brute strength, and they got in each other's way as they tried to overwhelm him and beat him down to the ground.

Longarm ignored Larry and concentrated on bloodying Lonnie's red, beefy face. He easily knocked aside a series of wild swings, stepped in close, and beat a quick, vicious left, left, right, left pattern on Lonnie's nose and eyes.

Larry tried to grapple him from behind, and Longarm twisted and drove the point of his elbow into the youngest Frye's face, splitting the youngster's lip and breaking his nose.

Louie was coming back up off the ground. Longarm ducked a looping, overhand right from Lonnie and kicked Louie in the face.

He heard a blubbery snort behind him and could sense Larry's rush to tackle him from behind. Longarm sidestepped and left one boot planted. Larry tripped over it and fell, rolling forward to cut Lonnie off at knee level and drop both of them into an untidy heap on the hard, gravelly soil.

The Frye brothers began screaming curses as they tried to untangle themselves.

"I done told you boys twice now, you don't use that kind of language." Longarm stepped forward as

32

Lonnie lunged upward. A forearm chopped into Lonnie's unprotected throat sent the bully back down on top of his brother.

Larry wriggled free of the pileup and tried to bolt away into the night, but Longarm grabbed him by the shirt collar with his left hand and clubbed him over the kidneys with a wickedly hard right fist. "You started this, damn it. Now stay and pay attention to what I'm telling you."

Louie was upright again and charging.

Longarm dropped the bawling Larry back on top of Lonnie, who by now was trying to find his feet again, and turned to meet the largest and presumably the oldest of the brothers.

Louie, dripping blood, ran full tilt into a swift uppercut that was hard enough to break teeth. Longarm could hear his jaw snap shut, and a moment later Louie was spitting blood from a new injury.

Longarm stepped back and surveyed the scene.

All three brothers were on the ground now. Lonnie hauled himself out from under Larry, who seemed uninterested in further efforts to rise, and wobbled his way toward the tall, lean stranger who did not have the good sense to be afraid of the name Frye.

Longarm shook his head. *Some people,* he thought, *are just too stupid to learn easy.*

He waited until Lonnie was positioned just nicely, then rattled Lonnie's brains—such as they were—with a left hook, right hook, and another left hook. Lonnie's head snapped back and forth like the tip end of a pennant in a stiff breeze. His eyes glazed and his knees buckled, dropping him straight down into a crosslegged position on the ground at Longarm's feet.

Lonnie leaned slowly back against Larry, who was

lying down with tears running down his face to mingle with the streaming blood.

Louie made a slow, weary attempt to get to his feet, then thought better of it and slumped down against the general pileup of battered Fryes.

Longarm was not even breathing particularly hard. "Boys," he said, "I really do want you to listen to me now." He smiled. "Are you listening?"

Louie nodded. So did Lonnie. Larry seemed too busy crying to pay particular attention at the moment. Longarm pointed at him. "Him too."

Lonnie took his baby brother by the shoulder and shook him somewhat harder than might have been strictly necessary. "Damn you, you little shit. You got us into this, now do what the man says."

Larry quieted down. His shoulders were still shaking with sobs, but at least he turned his head to look up at the tall man who loomed over the three of them.

"What it is, boys," Longarm said, "I'm a deputy U. S. marshal. I could put you in jail right here and now. I will too if that's what it takes. If you come at me again, I'm not going to mess with you. I'll just use up the cartridges in this Colt, and any of you that live through the experience, if there are any of you, I'll throw in jail. Assaulting an officer, maybe attempted murder. I know you've all seen those big gray walls at the other end of town. Mess with me again and you'll get a look at them from the other side."

Longarm squatted down beside the three silent and attentive Fryes and took his time about preparing and lighting a cheroot. The flame of the match was steady in his hand.

"You still listening? Good." He took a pull on the smoke. It tasted good. "What you should know," he said, "is that I'm around here from time to time. Every time I come, I intend to stop and see that Mrs. Armister and all her children are doing real good. You understand what I'm telling you, Louie? Lonnie? Larry?"

He waited until he had a nod of understanding from each one of them before he went on.

"If ever I hear that one of those children of Mrs. Armister *isn't* doing good, boys, I am going to hold the three of you personally responsible. And, boys, I mean if that lady or any one of her kids has been bothered by you, or by some other asshole from around here, or by the damn King of Araby, I am gonna hold the three of you responsible. I mean by any-fucking-body at *all*. You understand what I'm telling you now?"

All three bloodied heads nodded at once. Quickly.

"I mean, boys, the best interests of that lady and every one of her children are your best interests too. Anybody, *anybody* bothers them, ever, and it's *your* problem."

Longarm rose to his full height and clamped the end of his cheroot between his teeth. He reached up and readjusted the Stetson on his head. Somehow it had survived the fracas, which should only serve to add to the lesson.

"Now get your butts outa here," Longarm ordered.

Lonnie and Louie had to help Larry to his feet. The three of them staggered away into the night, lumped together to help support one another as they wobbled out of Longarm's sight.

Chapter 6

Patricia Armister was standing there when Longarm turned back from watching the Frye brothers disappear.

She was holding a long, hooked fireplace poker in her hands. It seemed an odd implement for her to be carrying until he realized she must have been there for some time, ready to help him fight the Frye boys if necessary. He swept his hat off and fidgeted with it.

"Ma'am," he said. "I'm . . . uh . . . sorry you had to see any of that. Or hear it."

"I understand, Mr. Long, but once again I am indebted to you. Or should I call you Marshal Long?"

"Whatever you find comfortable, ma'am. My first name is Custis. Most of my friends call me Longarm."

"Why didn't you tell me earlier?"

"About what I do?" He shrugged. "It didn't seem

36

important. Makes some folks nervous, I've found, so I generally don't say anything when I meet someone outside my line of work."

She nodded her acceptance of the explanation. Then she took a step closer and looked him over. "Come over here for a moment, Mr. Long. Into the light where I can see better."

Longarm did as he was instructed, and the pretty woman examined his coat and shirt front. She shook her head.

"What is it?"

She did not answer at once. Now she was examining his face as closely as she had just inspected his clothing. "At least it does not seem to be your blood," she said.

"What?"

"On your clothing. Right there. And there." She pointed. "You got it on you in the fight, I suppose." She shook her head again. "Such a shame. Very nice material, too. Come inside."

"I don't want to bother you, ma'am."

"Nonsense." She took him inside her home. "If those stains dry into the fabric and set, Mr. Long, you will never get them out. Off now. Let me have them."

She was tugging at his coat sleeves before he had time to protest.

Dutifully he removed the coat. She draped it over her arm and demanded the shirt as well. When he hesitated, she said, "Marshal Long. Really. I am a widow with three half-grown children. I have seen a gentleman without a shirt before."

He took the shirt off too.

Mrs. Armister took pity on him enough to find a towel he could drape over his shoulders. Then she disappeared into another room with the blood-stained clothing.

Longarm wanted another smoke, but two things prevented that. One was that he did not know if smoking would be allowed in this house. He would not have thought of lighting up in a lady's home without first securing her permission to do so. The other thing was that, for the time being, he had no cheroots. They had gone into the other room along with his coat and shirt. His vest, draped over the back of a chair, held only his watch and chain and derringer.

He contented himself with looking about the small room and what else he could see of the house.

The living room occupied most of the space inside the little place. It held a table and four chairs as well as a very few pieces of old but once fine furniture. Probably the room served the family for dining as well as sitting.

Shelves built of raw planking and brick, the brick mostly broken and some obviously used before, were filled with books, most of them leather-bound volumes with age-cracked spines and a look of much handling.

Overhead there was a loft with a counterweighted ladder. Probably where the children, at least the boys, would sleep. Matty more than likely slept with her mother in the tiny bedroom, scarcely big enough to contain an iron bedstead and a single small table that Longarm could see through an open doorway to the rear of the house.

Whatever else there was to the small structure Longarm could not see. That was where Mrs. Armister had taken his things, shutting the door behind her. He assumed that back there would be the laundry where she did her work. Probably, he thought, the area was also the kitchen, making use of the stove she would need to heat her wash water for the dual purpose of also cooking the family's meals.

The entire house, small though it was and lived in by four people, was tidy and spanking clean. Most of what he could see was of very good quality, but old, and some of it in need of repair.

Longarm helped himself to a seat at the table while he waited for Mrs. Armister to return.

He heard her moving about in the closed room at the back of the house. After a time she joined him again. She smiled. "It will take some time for those to dry," she said, "but I do not believe you will be able to see the spots. I think I got them in time."

"That's very kind of you, ma'am," Longarm said, rising.

"Oh, I almost forgot." Mrs. Armister went back into the room for a moment and returned with his cheroots and matches. She held them out to him. "I had to empty your pockets before I could clean the material," she apologized. "You might want one of these while we wait."

"It wouldn't offend you, ma'am? I could go outside to smoke. Or just take my things the way they are. I don't want to put you out, and they'd dry before morning."

"I would not think of it, Mr. Long. I have them on a rack near the fire. They will be ready directly. And of course I should not mind if you smoke. Aside from the fact that I owe you entirely too much to deny you the pleasure of a cigar, I happen to enjoy the smell. My late husband smoked, you see."

"Yes, ma'am." Longarm bit the end from a cheroot and lit up.

"You really do not have to keep calling me 'ma'am,'" she said with a smile. She sat across the table from him, and Longarm resumed his chair as well.

"Of course."

"Patricia would do," she said. She hesitated. "Longarm. That was what you said?"

"Yes, ma..." He smiled. "Patricia."

She looked into his eyes for a moment, and then away.

"Is something bothering you?" he asked.

She shook her head, but she blushed and still would not meet his eyes. She turned and reached back onto the bookshelf for a slender periodical. She used the magazine to fan herself.

"Are you all right? Really?"

"I...I shame myself, sir."

"Ma'am?"

"I...seem to be having thoughts that are not... appropriate."

"I don't understand," he said quite honestly.

She stopped fanning herself and sat with her eyes cast down toward the table surface. In a very small voice she said, "Matty told me you were frightfully handsome. She was right."

"Oh."

"I know I have offended you. And after you have been so kind to my family and to me. And I really should not have...a laundry woman...not suitable..." She started to cry.

Longarm did not know quite what to do. He left his chair and went around the table thinking to comfort her. But when he touched her shoulder, Patricia Armister turned and wrapped her arms around his waist and pressed her lips against the bare flesh of his belly. He could feel the heat of her tears.

He could feel something else too. The response was unwanted, but he could not deny it. After all, it was practically under the woman's nose.

She saw or felt or sensed Longarm's rising need. Trembling, as if doing it in spite of herself, she reached up to touch him and caress the thick, stiff length of him inside his trousers.

"I never . . . I have never . . . not since my husband died."

Longarm nodded. He understood. But gentlemanly inclinations can go only so far. And she continued to stroke and play with him through the cloth.

She had said the children had been sent away for the night.

He bent and scooped her into his arms and carried her toward the bedroom only a few paces away.

Her kisses—and her body—were fiercely hot. Eager.

There was no more reluctance. Not now.

They lay on the bed, writhing and pressing against each other, frustrated by the layers of clothing that separated them but unwilling to take the time to break apart. Not quite yet.

Patricia Armister made small noises deep in her throat, sounds of yearning and need, as Longarm explored her mouth with his tongue. While they kissed she clutched almost painfully at the erection that threatened to burst out through the buttons of his trousers.

With a groan of determined effort she broke away from him and rolled out of his grasp.

For a moment he thought she had changed her mind, that she wanted him to let her be. It was going to be difficult, but...

Instead she dropped to her knees beside the bed and began to tug at his boots, working them off and throwing them aside.

She pulled his socks off and bent to kiss and lick at his toes and across the top of his foot. Her tongue darted and flickered in between the toes. The sensation was extraordinary and completely unexpected. It was as if she could not feel or taste enough of his flesh now. As if once started there was no end to the satiation she would need.

She fondled his feet and sucked one of his big toes into her mouth, then fumbled with his belt buckle and fly buttons.

There too there was not enough for her to feel or to taste.

She cupped one hand under his scrotum to lift and tantalize his balls while her tongue laved the blood-red head of his tool.

She pulled him deep into her mouth, sucking with a painful, almost violent intensity.

"Better warn you," he rasped. "I'm awful close."

She withdrew only long enough to mutter, "Good," and went back to what she was doing, but more gently this time, deeper, thoroughly.

She drew him deep inside her mouth, down into the passage of her throat, and ran her still active tongue around the head while he was trapped inside her there.

Longarm usually had excellent control, but this was too much.

He shuddered and stiffened, arching himself forward deeper still into her eager throat, and spurts of hot fluid pumped out of him.

She stayed with him, draining him, pulling him to herself with hands and lips alike, until he was done.

Then, demanding, she released him and threw herself up onto the bed beside him.

She took his hand and pressed it over the moist, warm mound that had been empty far too long.

Longarm smiled at her.

His finger found the folded, furry lips of flesh and made their way to the entry, then dipped deep into her.

She gasped and raised her hips, spreading her knees wide and opening herself to him.

Longarm toyed inside her until his finger was thoroughly wet, then brought it back out and sought the small, elusive button of her pleasure.

He touched her there, stroked her and teased her.

Patricia Armister's lips pulled back into a grimace-like expression of uncontrolled sensation, and she moaned and raised herself forcefully against Longarm's moving hand.

He stroked her faster and harder on the exquisitely sensitive spot, and her hips began to move in time to the rhythm of his fingertip.

"Uhhhh-h-h-h-*AH!*"

She squealed a short, abrupt little scream of joy and release, and then she went limp against the bed.

After a moment she rolled her head to face him.

She was smiling. She gave the impression that that small effort of turning her head was all she had the strength to manage.

"So long," she whispered. "So good." She smiled again. "Thank you."

He smiled back at her. "If it's all the same to you, ma'am, I would just as soon not quit quite yet."

"Really? You mean you still can?"

He grinned at her.

Patricia Armister rolled over and nestled against the hard, masculine planes of his lean body. She sighed. "Thank you," she whispered again. And reached for him.

Chapter 7

It was nearly ten-thirty in the morning before Longarm finished breakfast at the same cafe where he had eaten supper the night before. He had slept unusually late, largely because it had been near dawn when he finally got back to his hotel room and was able to go to bed for the purpose of actual sleeping.

Not that he regretted the amount of time he had spent with Patricia Armister. Far from it. He still had a pleasantly hollow sensation south of his belt buckle and was filled with a slow, lazy lassitude that seemed to soften the colors and lightly blur the voices of those things and people around him on this bright and sunny day.

He paid for his meal, lighted a cheroot, and left the cafe.

The State Prison was on the west edge of Canon City, separated by only a few hundred yards from the commercial district of town.

He passed the warden's official residence, a tall, handsome house ornately finished with turrets and gables that sat on the near edge of the prison grounds. Several prisoners in their drab gray garb were working in the flower beds in front of the residence. No one seemed to be guarding them. On the other hand, the prisoners themselves seemed more interested in their work than in any escape plans. They did not so much as look up when Longarm passed them.

Longarm's credentials got him through the tall, iron-strapped gates and inside the prison walls. The guards passed him from hand to hand up the chain of command until he finally reached the office of a minor administrator. For probably the dozenth time, Longarm explained his business there.

"Oh, yes. I seem to remember something about that request." The man's expression indicated that he found the request unusual, even if his words did not. He shuffled through some of the many file folders piled in a basket on the corner of his desk and came out with the one he wanted. There was a note pinned to the cover of the folder. The man read it, grunted once, and asked, "D'you want to see him in an interview room or in his cell?" Apparently the way had been well cleared for the visit.

"Makes no difference to me," Longarm said. He reached for another cheroot. He really ought to cut down on smoking them, he thought, but they tasted so *good* this morning. Something to do, perhaps, with the flavors and the scents of Mrs. Armister still lingering in his senses.

"I would prefer that you do not smoke in here, Deputy."

Longarm grunted and shoved the cigar back into his pocket.

"In the cell would be easier for us," the administrator said. "Less manpower involved taking you to him instead of bringing him to you."

"I don't mind."

"You'll have to check your weapons. All of them."

Longarm nodded. "Here?"

"The guard will show you where."

The administrator fetched a secretary, who fetched a guard, and a few minutes later Longarm was admitted inside the cellblock section of the prison. He put his Colt and his knife into the lockable metal drawer where the guard indicated, but he kept the little .41 rimfire derringer in his vest. He had already searched his memory to determine whether he had used that hideout weapon when he arrested Sweeley those years earlier. As far as he could recall, the old man should have no knowledge about the gun, and Longarm simply felt better knowing he had one handy.

After much unlocking and relocking of stout doors and gates, Longarm was admitted to a courtyard. To his right was a massive building that housed the prison cells. They were of recent construction.

To his left was a long, lower line of older cells, tiny cubicles of stone and steel lined up against the base of a sheer rock wall, a natural formation of towering stone shaped something like an immense knife-edge lying on its side against the red soil. The massif was formed of a different kind of rock that was a dirty white color. The prison had been constructed butting up against it, using the rock wall hundreds of feet high as a natural barrier for one side of the prison grounds. The cells built against this wall were probably the oldest in the still growing prison. Prisoners contained there would get sunshine only in the early morning, and undoubtedly the cells were ferociously cold in the winter months. One of those would not have been Longarm's choice of living quarters.

The guard, armed with a billy club but no firearms, escorted Longarm to Sweeley's cell in that row and jangled his huge key ring to find the appropriate key.

Across the courtyard, several prisoners were idling in the sunshine. They eyed the guard and Longarm with curiosity. Longarm recognized several of the men, but neither he nor they extended greetings.

All of the prisoners left inside the gates at this time of day would be the hard-core, bad-ass boys, Longarm knew. The rest would be out working in the farm plots or dairy or engaged in road construction or whatever.

The guard swung the barred cell door open. "Call out when you're ready. I'll be out in the courtyard."

Longarm nodded and went inside, and the guard locked the door behind him.

Pop Sweeley had not changed since Longarm saw him last except for the change to prison clothing. And even that was not much of a change. Sweeley had not been a classy customer under the best of circumstances.

"'Bout time you showed up," Sweeley challenged him as soon as Longarm was inside the cell.

Longarm had equally fond feelings toward the old buzzard. "I still think they should have hanged you," he said.

Sweeley's head went back and he exposed a few rotting teeth in a grimace. Longarm assumed that it was the old bastard's idea of a laugh.

Longarm looked around the tiny cell. There was not much to see. The walls were solid stone and the ceiling sheathed in plate steel. There was a steel-framed cot with a thin mattress of dirty ticking and two blankets but no pillow. A hole in the stone flooring in the right rear corner served as a toilet. The only window was a very small one, and that heavily barred, set into the door.

"Home is where the heart is," Sweeley cackled. The laugh degenerated into a spasm of coughing that racked his thin frame. "Shit!" Sweeley muttered.

Longarm waited without sympathy until the fit of coughing ended. "What is it you wanted to see me about?" he demanded.

Sweeley sat on the edge of his bunk and cocked his head, squinting up at the tall deputy who had put him into this situation. "Don't like me much, do you, son?"

"Much? I don't like you at all. And if you call me 'son' again I just might trip and accidentally kick you in the balls when I fall."

Sweeley grinned. "Haven't changed, have you? Well, I hate your guts too, so that's fair enough."

"Is that what you wanted to tell me? Fine." Longarm turned away and began looking out the window for the guard.

"Wait, damn it."

Longarm turned back to face the old man again. He had to wait a bit until another spasm of coughing ended.

"I got something to say, damn you. Least you can do is give a dyin' man time to tell his story."

"You're dying, Sweeley? I hope you don't want me to hold your hand and tell you how sorry I am.

49

Far as I'm concerned, it's happening years too late."

Sweeley cackled again, and went into another bout of coughing. He rocked back and forth on the edge of the cot and gasped for air. "Yeah, you bastard," the old man said. "You ain't changed. I was counting on that."

Longarm waited him out.

"It's your fuckin' fault I'm dyin' now," he accused. "Got the damn consumption in this hellhole. Got no chance. They say if I don't die before fall I damn sure won't make it through next winter."

"Good."

Sweeley glared at him. "You're an unforgiving son of a bitch, Long. You always was."

"And you're a murderer and thief. So what has that got to do with why I'm here?"

"Because you're the hardest, meanest, sorriest bastard in the business, you prick. Because once you get onto something, you don't turn loose of it." Sweeley coughed twice and spat in the general direction of the slop hole in the corner of the room. "Because I've heard what the other boys say when they get in here too, and it's known that Deputy Custis F-for-fucking Long can't be bribed or bullied or led off a case once he gets onto it. That's why you're here, you bastard."

Sweeley grinned and cackled, this time managing to avoid the coughing. "And if you get yourself back-shot on this here case, prick, that'll be just fine too."

"You aren't making any sense."

"Huh. I reckon you know I had to rat on some o' my boys to keep my neck outa the noose a while back."

Longarm nodded.

"Well, I ain't so damn dumb that I told everything I knew," Sweeley said.

For the first time Longarm felt some measure of interest in the visit. His expression did not change, but now he was glad Billy had made him come.

"There was another feller involved. Big man, he was. Bigger now." Sweeley coughed into his fist. "Deal was supposed to be that I'd protect him, which I done. Then he was supposed to use his influence to get me the fuck outa here. Now he's got plenty of influence. But he ain't done shit toward getting me out. An' now it's too late. In this cell or any other damn place, you're lookin' at a walking dead man."

"So?"

"So I want my revenge, Long." He cackled and coughed. "Either way it works out, by God, I can have it. I put you onto this case an' you'll go after him. Either you get him, and I've got back at the son of a bitch, or he gets you, and I've got back at you, you prick."

Sweeley laughed loud and long, the nearly hysterical laughter choked aside finally by the coughing.

"If I'm *real* lucky," the old prisoner said, "he'll have you shot after you've done enough to nail his ass to the wall too. An' I hope to hell I live long enough to see it happen. That's the one hope I got left, thanks to you an' thanks to him. I just hope I live long enough to hear that it's happened."

Longarm folded his arms and leaned against the locked cell door.

"Tell me about it."

The name, when it came, was a bone-shaker.

Chapter 8

By the time Longarm finally called the guard to come let him out of Sweeley's cell, he barely had time enough to get his things from the hotel and make it to the railroad depot. He was glad he had had a late breakfast, because he did not have time for a decent lunch. He had to content himself with a cold, box lunch that he carried onto the train with him.

Longarm took a seat well away from the few other passengers on the eastbound coach and mulled over what Sweeley had told him.

Both his natural inclinations and his duty to the public he served put Longarm into the position of being an impartial observer in things like this.

He neither believed nor disbelieved. His job was to investigate and to determine the truth. Prove whatever the truth happened to be. Then, if necessary, act on that truth.

He tried not to allow himself preconceived opinions.

But one thing he knew for certain sure.

If Sweeley's statement was indeed the truth, shit was going to fly in all directions.

And if that happened, some of it was very likely to stick to Custis Long, William Vail, and possibly a good many others.

Longarm shook his head and opened the box lunch. Two dry-looking sandwiches, two shriveled apples that had been too long in storage, and a single limp pickle. He made a face and unwrapped the first sandwich. Why had he not thought this time to keep his carpetbag and bottle of rye in the passenger car with him? Once again the damn thing was back safely stowed in the baggage car beside his saddle.

Hiram Gort.

The name kept running through Longarm's head while he chewed mechanically on the sandwich. The pasteboard box probably would have tasted as good. But maybe today it was his taste that was off and not the sandwich. Certainly he had more than enough to think about right now.

He sighed.

Hiram Gort.

State Senator Hiram Gort.

The man known as the King of Brownstone.

Now gubernatorial candidate Hiram Gort, the man who in some circles was expected to become the next governor of the sovereign State of Colorado. And in those circles where Gort's election was not expected, it was at least thought he would be defeated only after a long and difficult fight.

Longarm shook his head again.

Again, by both personal inclination and sense of duty, Longarm took no partisan position when it came to politics.

But that could not be said of many others in government, including within the federal government. Including some of the people who could make life miserable for Marshal Billy Vail.

Vail, like Longarm himself and nearly everyone else in government service, held an appointed position.

Billy Vail was as straight-arrow as they came. If he had not been that kind of man, Longarm could not have stomached working for him all these years.

But the fact remained that Vail and Custis Long and countless others were ultimately accountable to people who thought that the machinations of politics was the primary force behind the rising and the setting of the sun each day.

Longarm shook his head and took another bite of dry sandwich. He had to look at the damn thing to see whether he was eating roast beef or sliced ham. It turned out to be beef.

The possible repercussions were not made any easier because Gort was a Democrat and the Republicans happened to be in power in Washington.

Billy Vail was ... Come to think of it, Longarm realized, he was not sure which party, if either, Billy Vail supported. It had never seemed important. Probably would not be now either.

But this was one of those things where you were damned if you did and damned if you didn't.

Politics was like that.

If they investigated Gort now, before the fall election, the Democrats would think they were doing it in an effort to help the Republicans. If Vail chose to wait until after the election, to make sure there was no suspicion about their motives for launching the investigation, the Republicans would want to know why the hell he had waited for months after a clear suspicion was raised about the Democratic candidate for the governor's chair.

Really, Longarm thought, whether Billy ordered the investigation now or in late November, whether Gort proved to be guilty or innocent—no matter what happened, some political son of a bitch was going to claim that it was the wrong move.

Obviously the Republicans would be happier if the man were proven guilty of Sweeley's allegations as quickly as possible. Ideally, before sunset this evening.

And the Democrats would be just as glad if he were cleared of the charges, but only after a delay until fall, so no doubts or suspicions would be raised among the voters.

And, no matter what happened, Billy Vail was going to be in the hot seat.

Longarm had his own guesses about what Vail would decide once he got word about Sweeley's charges.

Billy was straight-arrow.

He would take whatever heat came to him, and he would do his job the very best way he possibly could.

More than likely, Longarm thought, Vail would sit in his office with his chin high and tell his deputy to go ahead with the investigation, just let the damn chips fall wherever they might.

But, Longarm also knew, there was too good a chance that whatever decision Billy reached, the repercussions from the political professionals would come down right smack on top of Billy's balding head.

There was an awfully good likelihood that Billy Vail would not survive this investigation. That his job would not, anyway. Billy himself would, of course, but the odds were awfully strong that there would be a new United States marshal occupying the office in the Denver federal building weeks after Longarm's report was turned in.

Son of a *bitch,* Longarm would hate to see that.

As for his own job, he might be able to hang onto it when Billy left. But he would not want it. Not since the likelihood was all too strong that Billy would be replaced by some damned political hack like they had in all too many marshals' posts.

Long would not, *could* not, work under someone like that.

A free and honest hand was the only way to go in the life-and-death business of law enforcement.

Billy Vail always gave his men that. Many, perhaps even most, did not.

Longarm pondered the implications throughout the jolting ride past Florence to Pueblo.

When he changed trains to the standard-gauge northbound he put his saddle and rifle in the baggage car but brought the carpetbag into the smoking car with him. Several healthy pulls at the bottle of Maryland rye and another cheroot were comforting.

That did not help to solve anything, of course, but he enjoyed them just the same.

He thought about it some more while the D&RG train rolled north.

Hiram Gort.

Shee-it!

According to Sweeley, Gort was the organizer and

original leader of the gang, while Sweeley was his *segundo*, the only one the rank-and-file gang members ever saw or knew about.

But Gort had been part of it in the beginning, the old bastard had said.

Then, with some money in his jeans from his cut of the take, he had come out of nowhere to burst onto the scene at Brownstone. Made himself rich, made himself powerful, and then made himself a state senator and a rising power in Colorado politics by the simple expedient of maintaining absolute control over the lives of the voters in his home district.

From what little Longarm had heard about Gort in the past, it pretty well fit. Or, anyway, it *could* fit.

The true facts remained to be learned, but it certainly sounded possible.

Damn sure worth investigating in Longarm's opinion. No one, Republican or Democrat, wanted a murderer sitting in the governor's chair.

Damn, but Longarm wished he had paid more attention to state politics these past years. Maybe if he had he would have had a better handle on this thing.

Personally, Longarm did not give a damn whether Gort was innocent or guilty. He only wanted to be able to check out Sweeley's allegations—and that was all they were at this point, allegations—and then get on about the business he was paid to handle.

The pity of it as far as Longarm was concerned was that Billy Vail was the man in the middle. He was the one who was going to end up with shit on him regardless of what happened to Hiram Gort and Alfred "Pop" Sweeley.

When the train pulled into the station at Colorado Springs, Longarm got off.

Billy had said he could take a few days—well, maybe not days, but certainly some time—to see Ruth Morrisey.

Well, he intended to do that.

Even if he had not wanted to see Ruth, he would have been glad for any excuse to delay his return to Denver.

Custis Long was simply not ready to throw this one into Billy's ample lap. He wanted more time to think about it before he confronted his boss with Sweeley's accusations about the man who might well be Colorado's next governor.

Chapter 9

Reaching Ruth from Colorado Springs was more complicated than the few miles involved would indicate.

He had to lug his bag and saddle from the Denver and Rio Grande depot to the local terminal several blocks away, then pay a twenty-five-cent fare to ride in one of the open local coaches past Colorado City to Manitou, then unload his things there and find a hack and load everything into that.

But, he reflected, the effort would be worthwhile once he reached his destination.

The town of Manitou was set into a fold in the wall that was the Front Range. On three sides he could see the mountains rising high and ever higher, capped by Pikes Peak in the center of the semicircle. Off to the east could be seen the endless, rolling plains that ran all the way back to the Mississippi. The setting was nothing if not spectacular.

The town, small though it was, was full of well-dressed gentry who had come here for the mineral baths or to drink from the natural soda springs—odd, Longarm thought, that Colorado Springs should be so named, even though there were no springs nearer to it than Manitou's, which contained no mention of springs in the older community's name—or to enter one of the many sanatoriums that littered the hillsides above Manitou.

On the slopes above the town in nearly every direction he could see the white Sibley tents where the sanatorium patients lived in the fresh, health-giving mountain air. Small wonder that the establishments were busiest in the clement seasons, though. Winter in one of those tents would be rugged for the gentlefolk from the east who flocked here.

The hack rolled past the famous springs where now people came a thousand miles or more to drink the waters and where they still found Indian beads thrown into the springs as offerings from the times when another people had come here.

All around the springs there were vendors hawking souvenirs and drinks and foodstuffs.

A hotel keeper in Manitou, Longarm thought, would be a happy man.

The cab turned up Ruxton and then onto a narrow lane that climbed above the town, the single, plodding horse drawing it having to lean into the collar and work to make the grade.

Eventually they arrived at the destination Longarm had specified.

"Breath of Life Sanatorium," the driver announced. He held his hand out, palm upward. "That'll be a dollar, mister."

Longarm winced at the tourist-influenced tariff, but he paid. This, he was afraid, could not go on the expense account. He gathered his things and carried them toward the single real building he could see. Everything else was housed in tents.

He looked around as he walked. He had never been up here before. He had met Ruth when she was on a weekend shopping trip to Denver and had never had occasion to visit her at work or at home.

All around him there were patients taking the sun or the air, sitting in lounge chairs or groups around tables, playing card games or chess or simply reading in the sunshine.

The lower walls of most of the tents were rolled up, so he could easily see the living conditions of the patients. They were more sumptuous than he would have expected, with large beds and rugs spread over sawdust for flooring and bureaus and even lamps and easy chairs. It beat the hell out of any hospital Longarm had ever seen, yet the purpose was the same.

Not bad if a fellow could afford it, he thought.

Here and there some of the patients were being wheeled about in wheeled chairs pushed by young women wearing white smocks over their dresses and frilly, lace-edged caps to indicate their status as nurses. He had never seen Ruth in her working clothes. But then, he was really more interested in seeing her *out* of her working clothes.

He intended to ask for her in the office, but she spotted him before he reached the building.

Whatever she had been doing, he first saw her rushing across the graveled and smoothed but otherwise unlandscaped grounds to greet him.

She flung her arms around his neck and hung on,

dangling from him with her feet off the ground while she kissed him.

That answered that, Longarm thought. He was not going to have to pretend to be a long-lost brother or something. It was fairly obvious that she was not going to bother hiding him from her employers.

"Hello," he said once his lips were free.

"This is an unexpected surprise," she said brightly. She was still, however, hanging from his neck, making no contact whatsoever with the ground.

"I suppose I should have sent you a wire, but I wasn't sure when or if I could get here. Having a nice day?"

"A better one now, but yes, I am, thank you."

"Good." Longarm's hands were full of carpetbag and saddle. With Ruth still dangling from him he began to stroll through the sanatorium compound, whistling a light tune and making a show of looking at the surroundings. "Had dinner yet?"

"No."

"Off duty soon?"

"Fairly."

"Want to haul my ashes before or after?"

"Both."

"Okay."

Ruth laughed and let go of him. She dropped lightly to the ground and stood smiling up at him.

She had a fairly considerable way to look in that direction. She was barely five feet tall—Longarm suspected that she could not quite meet that height, because she absolutely refused to let him measure her— and could not have weighed more than ninety-five pounds. He had seen grade-school children who were larger.

In spite of her limited bulk, though, her figure was exceptionally fine, narrow-waisted—that she had let him measure once; she taped an incredible seventeen inches at the waist—and full of bosom and hip.

She was blonde, her hair done up in ringlets instead of the more common bun, with round cheeks and gray eyes. Her appearance was as sunny and glad as her disposition.

Since they had met, Longarm had taken a genuine liking to her.

She was an independent little scutter, though. Probably in her mid-twenties, she was unmarried, and she claimed she had no intention of marrying. She said she was having entirely too much fun as things were to spoil it all with marriage. Undoubtedly she had male friends other than Custis Long, but she never discussed them any more than Longarm was likely to tell her about the other women in his life. The casual, no-strings relationship they had fallen into seemed satisfactory to her; Longarm knew damn good and well it satisfied him.

She asked him to wait a few minutes while she took care of some things, then gave him another quick kiss and ran off to some other part of the sanatorium.

She was back within minutes. She smiled at him. "All taken care of."

"What?"

"My roommate, silly. I share a place with another girl who works here. I think she saw you when you got here. She sounded jealous, but she told me she could find another place to sleep tonight."

"I don't want to cause you any trouble."

"Trouble? Gee, I never heard it called that before." She linked her arm into his, having to reach up to do

63

so, and led him back the way they had just come.

"What about your work?" he asked.

"I took care of that too, sweetie. I have enough favors coming around here that we can sleep in late tomorrow morning too." She winked. "In case you have trouble getting to sleep tonight, that is."

"I have been feeling peckish lately," he said with a straight face. "Might need some nursing to get me through the night."

Ruth led him back down the lane a quarter mile or so, then turned off on a footpath that led downhill to the side of a small, bright-running stream that danced its way down out of the mountains.

There was a small cabin set in among the pines that grew beside the stream.

"Welcome home, dear," Ruth said. With her eyes dancing as brightly as the sun on the racing creek, she once again jumped up and hung from his neck. She opened the door for them and let Longarm carry her inside.

Chapter 10

Longarm smiled. "Nope. Couldn't possibly," he said. "Not so soon."

Ruth sighed and pretended disappointment. But damn it, Longarm thought, she had every right to be satisfied by now. Ruth Morrisey reached her climaxes faster and more easily than just about any woman Custis Long had ever been with. And she seemed to enjoy them with more sheer, unreserved pleasure as well. The damn girl must have gone through the throes of pleasure half a dozen times or more already. And *still* she wanted more.

She left the rumpled bed and brought him his cheroots and matches and an only slightly used saucer that would serve as an ashtray. "Weakling," she accused.

"Aren't you going to light this for me?" he asked, ignoring her comment.

"As the master wishes." She perched, quite fetchingly naked, on the side of the bed beside him and scratched a match aflame. She held it to the tip of the cheroot and kept it there until he nodded his acceptance of the bright glowing coal.

"Very good, sir." She carefully blew the match out, then dropped the still hot article onto his bare chest.

"Hey!" Longarm sat up abruptly, brushing the hot match away from his sweat-sheened flesh, but Ruth was already gone, disappearing into the other room of the small cabin.

She came back a moment later with a tray and cleared away the remnants of their supper.

Longarm's original intention had been to take her to one of the fine restaurants that catered to the tourist trade down in Manitou. But that, she had pointed out, would have involved several hours away from the bed. Entirely too much time, she had said. They could eat in instead.

That was before Longarm had discovered that Ruth did not cook. For all practical purposes, she was an innocent in the kitchen, however well experienced she might have been elsewhere.

So supper had been slices of cheese and salami and chunks of some kind of dark bread that Ruth's roommate favored, all of it taken in snatches while they rolled and romped on the narrow bed.

At first thought, Longarm had not thought much of the idea for a meal. But in actual practice it had been better than it sounded. Particularly the exercises undertaken between bites.

She cleared away what remained from the impromptu meal and disappeared into the front room again. This time when she returned she wore her frilly nurse's cap and light cotton smock—or whatever the thing was called—that was intended for wear over a normal dress.

At the moment, however, Ruth was not wearing anything else.

There were no sides to the garment. It came down in the front and rear like an over-large bib, and since she did not have it belted or fastened in any way, it did little to conceal the elegantly proportioned charms of her small but nonetheless lush body.

Longarm could not help laughing when he saw her. "You just don't give up, do you?"

She gave him a broad wink that was a parody of lewd suggestiveness and said, "Don't let up either, bucko."

Then, with a brisk professionalism he had never seen in her before, she clapped her hands sharply and ordered him to lie back on the bed.

"What the hell for?"

"Do as you are told, sir. Nurse is here now."

"What?"

"Roll over," she snapped.

"But . . ." Her hands were already guiding and pulling at him, turning him face down on the bed. What the hell, Longarm thought, he might as well go along with the game, whatever it was supposed to be. He rolled over.

Ruth began to run strong, well-practiced hands over the planes of his shoulder muscles and down his back. Her touch was firm and professional, with no hint of caress in it. "This is for your own good," she said.

It did feel nice, Longarm admitted to himself. Relaxing and pleasant. He wondered if this kind of thing was part of what she did for her patients at the sanatorium.

After a minute or so, Longarm realized that he could feel something back there *other* than Ruth's firm, sure hands.

There was something else.

He tried to turn to see, but she reached out and stopped him.

"Let nurse handle this, if you please."

"Yes, ma'am," Longarm said with a chuckle. He flopped down face first again and lay still.

But, damn it, he was sure now that there was something else . . .

He smiled.

A flicker here. A hint of contact there. Lightly, ever so lightly at first, so that he had not even been sure he was able to feel it, there was the soft, warm, moist flutter of her tongue against his back.

And all the while she continued to give him that firm, impersonal massage.

Now that he knew what he was feeling, though, he was barely aware of the touch of her hands.

Her tongue licked here, reappeared there, touched briefly in one spot, and then lingered in another.

Somehow she managed to do that without seemingly changing the angle or the effort of her hands pressing and kneading him so professionally. She must be a contortionist in addition to her other accomplishments, Longarm decided.

The hands moved lower, into the small of his back, and the tongue moved lower still.

It darted with devastating effect into the crack of

his ass, remained there only a moment, and then moved still lower.

He could feel her breath hot against him as her tongue worked with speed and precision to penetrate him and circle the extraordinarily sensitive area.

In spite of himself, Longarm was feeling a fresh surge of excitement now. He honestly had thought he was done for until morning, but apparently Ruth knew better about that subject than he.

She finally gave up the pretext of the massage and spread the cheeks of his butt aside with her hands to give herself an easier access to the target of that flickering tongue.

After a moment she licked her way slowly down, across the almost painfully sensitive zone between his ass and his balls, until she was licking the limp, wrinkled sack of his scrotum.

Longarm had to clench his teeth to keep from crying out. It felt that good.

He was fully erect again now. Ruth seemed to know that. She rolled him onto his side and reached around his waist to fondle and toy with his cock while she continued to lick his balls.

Longarm thought he could hear a soft chuckle when she touched him and knew that he was hard again.

She pulled one ball into her mouth and held it there for a moment, the heat of her body sinking into him and intensifying the feelings. She allowed that ball to slip out of her lips and gently, very gently, drew the other in.

This time Longarm did groan.

She pulled him over until he was lying on his back and scrambled out from under him. She was still wearing her cap and that silly bib thing, he saw.

She lay on top of him, straddling his chest, and bent to mouth the base of his cock. Her breath was hot and moist on him there.

Slowly, nipping and sucking gently with her lips, never once allowing her teeth to touch him, she worked her way carefully up his shaft until her open mouth was poised over the head of his now throbbing member.

She laughed lightly, then lowered her head over him, trapping and engulfing him in her heat.

Longarm groaned and raised his hips to her. He could feel the ring of tight muscle at the back of her mouth. There was a slight resistance there, then even greater heat as the head of his cock slipped out of her mouth and beyond, into the slim column of her throat.

She accepted him with apparent comfort and adjusted her position on top of him, wriggling backward on his chest until her own gaping, wet sex was poised at his chin.

Her demand was plain. She liked to get as well as to give.

Longarm gave her what she wanted.

Within seconds he could feel her tighten up, her entire body going rigid and the cheeks of her pert little ass, only inches above his nose, clenching in.

She shuddered and moaned and writhed against him in her climax.

She pulled away from him for a moment and cried out.

Then, relaxed, she dipped her head and once again engulfed him, this time working with long, sure strokes to pull him to the brink of release.

She let him hang there for a moment, her mouth

and tongue immobile, then sent him spilling over the edge of release, hot sperm spewing out into her throat.

She stayed with him for several leisurely moments, then slowly let him slip free of the heat and wetness of her.

"No more, huh?" she asked. "Couldn't possibly, huh?" She laughed.

"I reckon," he said, "that my nurse knows best."

Chapter 11

Longarm bent low to kiss Ruth goodbye. "I'm glad I came," he said.

"Are you *sure* you will be busy this weekend? Are you positive you can't make it back here like we planned?"

He shrugged. "Work. You do understand, don't you?"

She made a face, but she nodded.

"Good. I'll see if I can get a few days off as soon as this thing is cleared up."

He kissed her goodbye again, picked up his gear, and began walking down the mountainside toward Manitou.

Now if things only went as smoothly for the next few days, well, there was at least a chance that he could preserve Billy Vail's job for him.

Although Longarm did not really expect Billy to

be totally appreciative when he discovered—as eventually he would have to do—just how Vail's top deputy intended to accomplish that.

The answer, or a possible one anyway, had been in his mind when he awakened this morning.

If Longarm went back to Denver and reported in to Billy about Pop Sweeley's charges against Senator Hiram Gort, there was sure to be hell to pay.

Once he had slept on the problem, the solution seemed perfectly obvious: Don't report back to Billy.

Not a damned word of it.

What Billy Vail did not know could hurt him, of course. It could wind up hurting Deputy Custis Long even worse. But it sure seemed better than the alternatives which still looked to be awful. If this idea was poor, anything else he could think of would only be worse.

He just would not go back to Denver.

Hell, when he didn't show up, Billy would only assume Longarm had stopped in Manitou and forgot himself for all the playing Billy would think he was still doing with Miss Morrisey. Longarm had been pretty careful about his job lately. Surely he could be forgiven a small, self-granted leave of absence on the eve of a long holiday weekend.

Longarm grinned to himself and continued down the lane to the foot of the mountains.

As soon as he reached Manitou he found a cafe and treated himself to a huge breakfast. He had passed Ruth's offer back at the cabin. Cold salami made a fine lovers' feast late in the evening. It had not sounded so appealing in the dawn's early light.

He gorged on steak and fried potatoes *and* a stack of fluffy griddle cakes for breakfast, then took the next local back to Colorado Springs and the main-line connection.

The Denver and Rio Grande carried him back to Denver. Instead of getting a hack to take him into the city, though, Longarm walked the short distance to another rail terminus, hoping all the while that he would see no one he knew, that no one would see and recognize him. He did not want Billy Vail to get any hint that he was back in town.

The Denver, Brownstone and Pacific—rather wildly optimistic in its name, since it was a shabby little short-line railroad serving the freight needs between Denver and Brownstone to the southwest—had its depot in a poorly converted livery barn on the south side of Cherry Creek.

Its afternoon train was already made up, running virtually empty with a single passenger coach, which looked like it had been in service approximately three weeks longer than there had been railroads in the United States, and a string of flatcars. Nearly all of the freight on the line was carried from Brownstone back to Denver. There was little need for traffic in the other direction.

Longarm was early for the scheduled departure, so he had a cup of passable coffee at the depot but decided to wait before he ate again. The sandwiches he had gotten back in Canon City had cured him of that vice for the time being.

When the conductor announced the train ready to leave, Longarm showed his identification in lieu of a ticket and climbed into the rickety coach. By doing so he deprived the line of a full twenty percent of the passenger revenue they should have expected from the afternoon run.

The distance to Brownstone was slightly less than twenty miles by rail, but even so the train took more than an hour to get there.

When they finally arrived, Longarm took a good look around. He had never been to the town before, although of course he had heard of it.

Nothing he saw surprised him.

Along the Front Range mountains, tucked up against the base of the foothills, there are found large but infrequent deposits of sandstone and limestone ranging in color from the oyster white that the State Prison was built up against to the almost garish red found in Red Rocks near Denver or the more famous Garden of the Gods between Manitou and Colorado Springs. Similar deposits, small and more numerous, are scattered along the foothills and out onto the grasslands to the east. For some reason most of them were laid down in great, huge slabs tilted skyward at an acute but not completely vertical angle. Most tilted slightly toward the west.

Brownstone was one of the largest such deposits. The town was built on and around a massive, dark red stone formation that for years now had been quarried for building stone. Much of Denver was built from it. More had been sent east over the years to provide facing stone for office buildings and expensive homes in the swank sections of places as far away as New York City and Boston.

As far as Longarm could see, there was not a whole hell of a lot about Brownstone that was swank.

The railroad depot at this end was even shabbier than the DB&P terminal at the Denver end, and the buildings around it did not look much better.

There were only a few streets in the town. The

business district consisted of several lines of unpainted wooden buildings, none of which was more than two stories high. The homes he could see were built of milled lumber or, those closest to the business area and presumably the oldest, of logs. Nowhere did he see any evidence of construction with the red stone that had given Brownstone its reason for existence. Odd, Longarm thought. Probably the quarried material was thought to be too expensive and valuable to waste on the home folks when it could be sold at a high profit elsewhere.

There was plenty of the material in sight, though. The railroad tracks across from the depot were lined with neat stacks of stone already cut, shaped, and smoothed for use as a stone veneer somewhere.

And nearly everything he could see, including even the leaves on the few trees in sight, was coated with a thin layer of red dust from the quarrying. Longarm thought he could almost taste the stone dust in the air he breathed here. He began to hope this job would not take too long. He was already anxious to get back to Denver and then, as quickly as possible, back to Ruth for that promised holiday.

He shouldered his saddle, picked up his carpetbag, and went to find the nearest hotel.

The nearest hotel turned out to be also the only hotel in Brownstone. Some clever entrepreneur with a gift for words had named it the Brownstone Hotel. Longarm was impressed.

On the other hand, the Brownstone Hotel really was a much finer establishment than he would have expected, judging from the rest of the town. The exterior was as dusty and weathered as all the other buildings in town, but the lobby was ornate with floral axminster carpeting, gilt-framed mirrors, crystal chandeliers, and what looked to be hand-painted ceiling panels. The lobby was also quite full of gentlemen and their ladies dressed for a near-formal holiday.

Longarm shouldered his way through the streams of moving people, catching a word or a phrase here and there that mostly had to do with either politics or stock issues, and concluded that this was a much wealthier and more genteel crowd than he ever would have expected to find in a quarry burg.

He reached the desk clerk and requested a room.

"Sorry, sir. We been booked full for this weekend, oh, for a month or better now."

"Whatever for?"

"Senator Gort, sir. Surely you know he's running for governor this fall."

Longarm nodded.

"Fourth o' July weekend, sir, is when the campaignin' gets serious. Why, half the Democrats an' three-fourths of the newspapers fellas from Denver will be here this weekend to hear the senator make his speeches."

"Damn," Longarm muttered. Even though he had spoken softly, an aging matron standing half a dozen paces away turned to glare at him. The desk clerk did not look pleased either. "Sorry," he added.

"I believe you should leave now, sir," the clerk suggested.

"There's no hope at all for a room?"

"Absolutely not."

Damn it, Longarm thought. He considered showing the man his badge and making the request an official one. But the clerk's swiftly changing disposition after

Longarm's minor indiscretion only made it seem likely that an official request would give the man that much more pleasure in turning him away. Besides, in a crowd like this, a deputy marshal's badge would be small potatoes indeed.

Longarm thanked the man as civilly as he could, picked up his things, and shouldered his way back out through the crowd of political swells.

Out on the street, back in the heat and the rock dust, Longarm stood on the board sidewalk looking indecisively up and down the street.

"Carry that bag for you, sir?"

"What?" Longarm looked down at the little boy who had spoken. The kid was not more than seven or eight. He looked scarcely big enough to drag the carpetbag. In his preoccupation, Longarm had not even noticed him standing by the front steps to the Brownstone Hotel.

"I ast could I carry your bag, sir."

Longarm smiled at the dark-haired little boy. "I'd hire you for that, son, except I don't have a place for you to carry it to."

"No room, huh?" the kid said with a quick grin.

"That's right."

"You could pay for a room, huh?"

"Of course."

The little guy's grin got wider. "Much as a whole *quarter?*" He sounded like the thought of a whole *quarter* would have seemed to him like half the supply of money in the known world.

"Oh, I think possibly so," Longarm said.

"We got a spare room," he said proudly. "Bet my mama'd let you use it if you could pay."

"Do you really think so?"

He nodded solemnly.

"We could ask her," Longarm said.

The kid grinned again. "Want me to carry your bag an' show you the way?"

Longarm chuckled and gave the little fellow the carpetbag. "When you grow up, son, you're going to make quite the salesman."

The grin widened, then returned to its normal happy state. "My name's Anthony Alberto DeLuca the Third. You c'n call me Tony if you want." He headed off down the street, lugging the carpetbag, with Longarm trailing slowly at his side.

"And my name is Custis Long, but you can call me Longarm, Tony."

Dark eyes flashed gratefully up at him at the favor of being allowed to call a grown-up by name.

Tony chattered his way down the short length of the street and beyond, down a sharp slope Longarm had not been able to see from downtown Brownstone. The slope was covered with shacks scattered around like windblown litter. Few of them were nice enough to have earned the title "house."

While they walked, the little boy explained that Papa was sick and couldn't work in the quarry any more until he got well, so Mama was keeping the family and Tony was helping her. He sounded proud of that, and Longarm suspected that Tony's having bagged a paying guest for overnight was a large part of that pride.

The farther they walked, though, the less certain Longarm was that he should have accepted the little boy's offer.

Still, he would have to spend the night somewhere, if only on a hard bench in the railroad depot waiting for the morning train back to Denver, and he could at least take a look at the house and talk to the mother. If the place looked less comfortable than a train station bench, he could always go back.

When they got there, though, the house was a surprise. It was larger than the shacks they had been passing and was solidly built of very carefully laid stonework.

Tony stopped short of the house and set the carpetbag down for a rest. He surveyed his house with a pride that equalled that he had already shown.

"My grandpa built our house," he said.

"Really?"

Tony nodded. "He came over a long time ago. He was a stonecutter in Italy. He was already real old when he came here. He built the house an' sent to New York City for Grandma, but he was real old, so I never knew him. He died, you know."

"I didn't know," Longarm said.

Tony picked up the bag and headed toward the house again, with Longarm following.

Tony reached the house and marched inside, dragging the carpetbag and his guest along with him. Longarm followed hesitantly, unsure of the reception he would find here.

The little boy set the bag down in the hallway beside a door leading into a small, over-furnished parlor, and raced ahead through another doorway into the back of the two-story house. "Comp'ny, Mama," he was calling. "I found a man to pay for a room, Mama."

Longarm removed his hat and waited where he was.

The woman who came into the hall, wearing an

apron and wiping her hands on a towel, was hardly what he would have expected to find in a place like Brownstone.

She was breathtakingly beautiful, with glossy black hair and dark, flashing eyes. Her complexion was that of fresh cream and her figure frankly exciting. She did not, however, look particularly pleased to see this unexpected visitor.

"Ma'am," Longarm said.

"Tony tells me you will pay a whole quarter for the use of our home." Tony had come into the doorway behind her. She handed him the towel she had been using and shooed him back into the kitchen.

Longarm smiled. "The amount was his suggestion, ma'am. I really do need a room for a night or two, but I think the rate should be negotiable."

Mrs. DeLuca smiled. "I see." She had a slight accent, which Tony seemed to have escaped. She sighed. "We could use the money, God knows. And I hear the town is full. You could pay in cash?"

"Yes, ma'am."

"Dollar a night?" When he hesitated only a fraction of a second, she hurriedly added, "With meals." Apparently the family needed the money quite badly.

"Actually, ma'am," Longarm said, "the usual rate is two dollars a night." He smiled. "With meals, that is." He stretched things only a little there, and, hell, it was expense-account money.

Mrs. DeLuca's expression brightened considerably. She looked . . . Longarm had to search for the word for a moment before he realized . . . she looked relieved. He had to wonder just how much help a couple of extra dollars could be.

She turned and said something in rapid Italian, and

for a moment Longarm thought she had just launched a flood as more DeLucas tumbled through the doorway to meet and to inspect him.

When the confusion settled down, he could see that there were only Tony and three smaller children, two boys and a toddling girl, and a very handsome, full-bodied, dark-haired woman of forty or so. It took Longarm several minutes to realize that the older woman was the Grandma Tony had talked about.

As soon as those introductions had been made— he never did get the names of all the children straight— the little girl took him by the hand and led him in a ground-floor room to the right of the hallway to meet Papa.

Apparently the room had been converted to a bedroom from some former use. It was dark and had a closed-up, musty smell of illness and stale air. The curtains were drawn over the windows, and it took Longarm a moment for his eyes to adjust to the relative darkness.

Papa DeLuca turned out to be a slim, olive-complected young man who could not have been more than twenty-five at the most. He probably had been a handsome man once, but now he looked drawn and wasted, his cheeks sunken and his movements weak.

Even so, he smiled with real joy when his children came tumbling into his room, and he greeted Longarm with an accent so heavy it was difficult for Longarm to make out what he was saying. With the children he chatted happily in Italian.

The introductions were made, such as they were, and Longarm was led back out of the bedroom and upstairs to a large, virtually bare spare room. He thought that it probably had been the DeLucas' own

82

room until illness made them move everything downstairs for Papa's convenience. Longarm's carpetbag and saddle were already placed neatly in a corner.

"I will move a bed in," Mrs. DeLuca said. She looked embarrassed. "We have sold what we could, you understand."

Longarm knew that finding a spare bed here would mean some of the children or even Grandma DeLuca would have to be moved. "Just a pallet is all I need, ma'am."

She protested, but he managed to assure her that he was accustomed to sleeping on the ground, and a pallet would be much more comfortable than a too-soft bed.

"Has your husband been sick very long?" he asked as he followed her downstairs.

She looked troubled. "Sick. *Pah!* He was strong, healthy man. Then a scaffold broke. The rocks, they fall. Hit him in the chest." She slapped her own quite shapely chest by way of emphasis. "He doesn't get better, can't work now, so they fire him. No more job, no more money. But he still got a family to feed. Bastards. They don' care."

Longarm said something sympathetic and joined the family at the table for a meal that was surprisingly tasty, especially considering that it had pasta and rice and sauces but no meat whatsoever in the fare. He ate very little.

As soon as the supper was over, he thought, he could walk back up to Brownstone and buy a steak. Besides, he needed to talk with Senator Gort. He wanted a chance to meet the man and size him up. Sometimes a direct confrontation was the best way to go about that.

Chapter 12

The door was opened by a huge black man who loomed several inches above Longarm's own considerable height and who had the muscles to match his size. He was wearing a dark suit, starched white shirt, and white bow tie, and he looked formal as well as formidable. Behind him the sounds of music and conversation and the number of people and lights in evidence indicated that a party or function of some sort was in progress.

"You are late, suh," the butler apologized. "The dinnuh has ended, an' the gennelmen are having cigahs an' brandy. May I inquiah your county an' precinct, suh, so's I can announce you?"

Longarm grunted. Apparently he had blundered into some gathering of political wardsmen or some such thing here.

He showed the butler his credentials and said, "But

I don't want to bother the senator if he's busy. I could come back. I wanted to go get a bite to eat anyway. I could do that first."

The butler gave him a half-bow and said, "I am sure, suh, the senator will be pleased to receive you as soon as he is able. If you care to wait heah, suh, there is much left from the senator's repast. You c'n eat while you wait, suh."

Longarm thanked the man and followed him into the back part of the huge house. The other guests, most of them dressed quite elegantly, ignored him when they saw that the butler was leading him back toward the kitchen and not into the crowd.

Finding Senator Hiram Gort's home had been no problem at all. It was the one truly fine structure in Brownstone, three stories high and built of the famous red rock. Porches—verandahs, Longarm supposed they would be called here—encircled the ground floor, and there was no expense spared for lamp oil and candles to turn night into day throughout the house and for yards around it. The furnishings were conspicuously fine—and expensive.

The butler showed Longarm into the kitchen and motioned him toward a long oak table piled high with platters of leftovers from the dinner that had been held here this evening. Two plump, dark-haired women were busy cleaning up after the meal.

"Help yourself to whatever you would enjoy, suh. The senator shall be free presently."

"Thanks."

The butler bowed his way out, and the two women eyed Longarm while pretending not to. They said something to each other in Italian, but did not speak directly to Longarm. After a moment Longarm found a clean plate and dug into the feast of roast beef, glazed duck, and half a dozen main dishes that were left over from the banquet. He was long since satisfied before the senator finally made his appearance.

Gort bustled into the kitchen wearing formal clothes. He had to introduce himself, though, before Longarm realized who he was. He did not look at all like Longarm's idea of a politician.

Hiram Gort looked like a roughstring rider dressed up and plunked down into the midst of high society. He was shorter than average, whipcord slender, and sun-wrinkled around the eyes and mouth. He was probably in his mid-fifties now, but he looked like he would be able to fork a wild bronc and ride it down without raising a sweat.

Probably, Longarm thought, the man had never seen a mustang close up, but he nevertheless had that look about him.

"My man tells me you are a United States marshal," Gort said pleasantly enough. "Out of Denver? That would make you Vail, right?"

Longarm corrected him.

"Of course, Deputy." Gort smiled. "Sorry to keep you waiting, but I'm sure you understand."

Longarm smiled and assured the politician that he did indeed understand.

"Good." Gort motioned Longarm back to the chair he had been using while he waited. The state senator pulled another chair out from the table, turned it, and straddled it, leaning his forearms on the back of the chair and peering across it toward his guest. "Now, Deputy Long, what can I do for you?"

"I wanted to ask you a few questions, sir, about a man named Sweeley." Longarm watched closely for the reaction to that name.

"That son of a bitch!" Gort exploded. "What's he been up to now?"

"You do know him then, sir?"

"Know him? Hell, no, I don't know him. But I sure know *about* him. Miserable old bastard. Do you know what he's been doing, that sorry old shit?"

"No, sir, but I was hoping you would tell me." He hoped neither of the women who were still at the sink washing dishes could speak English. Or that their employer would watch his language.

"Huh!" Gort said. "Well, you're damned right I'll tell you. And thank goodness someone has finally gotten that boss of yours to help me get that old bastard off my back."

Apparently, Longarm realized, Gort thought he had been sent for some specific purpose of helping. That was nice, Longarm thought, even if untrue. But then again, Billy had hinted that there was some political pressure being applied about that trip down to Canon City. So maybe Gort knew more about this than Longarm did.

"Yeah, I'll tell you," Gort was saying. "It started . . . hell, I don't know. Months ago. Maybe late last year some time. Mind you, I've never laid eyes on this Sweeley fellow. Wouldn't know the man if I sat down to the table with him. But he came up with my name from somewhere, all right." Gort reached into his pocket for a pipe, loaded it, and took his time about lighting it.

"The cheeky bastard started writing me letters, demanding—mind you, he wasn't *asking* me, the son of a bitch was *demanding*—that I arrange a parole for him. Why, he never did say, but he must have written

87

to me half a dozen times or more. I had my secretary answer him, of course. At first with the standard letter asking why he thought he deserved consideration for parole. Sent copies to the appropriate state people. All the usual sort of thing." He waved his hand negligently, as if Longarm should know what the usual sort of thing was.

"All this Sweeley fellow did was write back and demand a parole again," Gort went on. "Hell, man, I'm not even on any committees that would get into anything like that. Of course, it was already an open secret that I would be running for governor this year. So I assume he was thinking I would win the race." Gort flashed a smile and added, "Can't say that I hope he's wrong about that, now can I? And he wanted to be first in with a request for clemency or what have you. If that's what he wanted, he is damn sure gonna be disappointed, let me tell you. After I saw a few of those letters, I had his record checked out. Son of a bitch shoulda been strung up on the nearest cottonwood is the way I see it. Clemency? Shit. When I get to be governor, Deputy, I might ask for a retrial and a hanging, but I won't give the man any damn clemency."

Whatever Gort's pre-politics background, Longarm thought, he had not been a lawyer. The guarantees against double jeopardy would protect Sweeley from any chance of a retrial and stiffer penalty regardless of what any state governor might want.

"And then do you know what the old bastard did?" Gort asked indignantly. "When I wouldn't make him any promises about a parole, he started writing to the newspapers about me. I assume you have read those letters."

"No, sir, I'm afraid I haven't."

"You ought to. You really ought to do that," Gort said. "Letters to the editor. Papers all over the damn state have gotten them. Open letters addressed to me. Why, some of the damn things have actually reached print." Gort sounded offended by the idea that any editor would have printed such a thing without Senator Gort's permission and approval.

"What did those letters say, Senator?"

"The same shit," Gort said. "Demanding a parole. Some of them hint that I *owe* him a parole. Bullshit like that." Gort shook his head. "A thing like that could give people the wrong idea, Deputy. Let me tell you, in an election year, any fucking thing can give people the wrong idea. I can't have that, you know. Not at all. Not this year, especially. It's one thing to expect to carry my own district here," he admitted. "It is quite another when the vote is statewide. Quite another." He puffed on his pipe and calmed himself a little. He had begun to get rather red in the face.

"What I want you to do, Deputy," he said, "is for you to go down there to that prison, wherever the hell it is, and have a word with this man Sweeley. I want you to put the fear into him. Make him understand that if he keeps this up, things will go poorly with him. Do you understand me, Deputy? I want you to get this bastard off my fucking back."

Apparently State Senator Gort saw nothing wrong with ordering a federal employee about on a mission to Hiram Gort's benefit.

Interesting, Longarm thought. But then, there were some national ramifications to what party held which state houses, he suspected. Although politics was not something Custis Long paid a whole hell of a lot of attention to.

"You never knew Sweeley in the past?" Longarm asked. "Before his conviction?"

Gort grunted. "Never heard of the son of a bitch until he started sending those letters."

"Are you aware that Sweeley is now saying that you were his silent partner when he was operating the crime ring and committing those murders?"

"The hell you say." Gort certainly sounded genuinely surprised.

"I'm afraid so, Senator."

"Jesus Christ, he hasn't been putting shit like that in some more of his letters, has he?"

"No, sir. I've already been to the prison. I talked with him there."

"Jesus Christ," Gort repeated. "The man could ruin me if something like that gets around before the election." He shook his head. "I want you to go back down there, Deputy. I want you to impress on this man Sweeley that he should lay off. Or something very unpleasant could happen to him. Very unpleasant."

"I don't believe I could do a thing like that, Senator."

Gort glared at Longarm. Then, almost before the hard expression had time to register, he softened and apologized with butter-smooth ease. Longarm was not really listening to what Gort was saying then, though. He was thinking that the man was good, very good,

90

but Longarm did not believe the buttering-up for a moment. Gort was still as thoroughly angry as he had been. He was merely trying to cover himself now with this federal officer who was not and never would be directly under his control.

"Of course you could not," Gort said. "Of course not. But I really am concerned. You must understand that, Deputy. This man could absolutely ruin me in the election, and I have never heard of him until recently."

"Of course, sir."

"You will help me, then? However you can?"

"Of course, Senator."

"Good. Very good." Gort stood and knocked his pipe dottle out on the edge of a platter containing enough cold roast beef to feed the DeLuca family for a week of better eating than they had in ages.

The senator shook hands with Longarm and excused himself. "Must get back to my guests, you know. We are discussing my campaign schedule, you understand. Have a lot of speeches and stops to line up and very little time to do it all. Have to press the flesh and kiss the babies." He laughed. "All that bullshit. But it works, Deputy. That's the thing to remember. That is what wins an election."

"Yes, sir. Thank you for taking the time to see me."

"You'll be going back to see that fellow Sweeley now, will you?"

"Possibly. I really don't know yet."

"See that you do, Deputy. There . . . uh . . . may be a way I can express my appreciation. After the election. If you know what I mean."

Gort left the kitchen before Longarm had a chance to suggest that he fuck one of the glazed ducks on the table.

Longarm looked at the two Italian women who were so industriously engaged in dishwashing. He resisted an impulse to apologize to them for their employer and let himself out the back door of the Gort mansion.

Chapter 13

On the way back to the DeLuca house, which he had a little difficulty finding in the dark, Longarm stopped briefly at the Brownstone Hotel's bar and their restaurant. The bar had Maryland rye, which they were willing to sell by the shot, and the restaurant had the better part of a ham left over from the evening dining, which they were willing to sell also. Longarm enjoyed the rye on the spot and carried the ham along with him to the DeLuca place.

Mrs. DeLuca was still awake, sitting in the small parlor with a book in her lap, but there was no sign of the rest of the family.

"Evening, ma'am," Longarm said. "I hope you weren't waiting up for me."

"No," she said, although Longarm suspected it was a fib. "This is the only time I have quiet in the house."

"Listen, ma'am, I'm hoping you can help me out with something."

"Yes?" She looked suspicious about the request to come.

"While I was over at the hotel, ma'am, I got into a card game with some fella, and along about the time he should have quit but wouldn't, he put this into the pot. And I, well, I kinda won it. I wondered if you could use it, since I sure can't." He held out the paper-wrapped bundle of ham. It had been a whole ham, a large one, and there were probably still eight or ten pounds of meat on it, cooked and ready to eat.

"What is it?" The woman, still young and very pretty in spite of the number and frequency of the children she had borne, took the package and began to unwrap it.

Before she had it open she knew what it was. The strong, pleasing scent of the meat escaped almost as soon as the first layer of paper was pulled back. She began to cry.

"I'd sure appreciate it, ma'am, if you'd take that off my hands," Longarm said.

She gave him a look that mingled disbelief with real joy, then, sobbing, bolted back toward the kitchen. She left the ham there and then ran into the bedroom she shared with her broken husband.

After a moment Longarm could hear the man's thickly accented voice calling out to him. "Yes?" He went reluctantly to the doorway. Hell, he had not intended to cause this kind of fuss.

The man spoke rapidly to him in a brand of English that managed to sound like Italian. The message was clear, though. Longarm thought that a simple "thank you" would have been enough.

"This is wonderful," his wife was saying over and over. "The children, they have not had meat in so

94

long now. An' Tony, the doctor says he needs to have his strength, but what we can afford does little for him."

"Like I said, ma'am, you'd really be doing me a favor if you'd take the thing off my hands. That's all it means to me is a favor to get rid of it."

She laughed and shook her head, but she did not do him the discourtesy of actually saying that she did not believe him. After a moment she disappeared back toward the kitchen, while her husband continued to express his thanks from his position on the bed.

Hell of a shame, Longarm thought, for such a nice young fellow to come to a condition like that.

Mrs. DeLuca returned quickly with a small plate of thickly sliced ham and some hard, crusty bread-sticks. She offered them first to Longarm.

"No, thank you, ma'am. I had all that at supper, and then over at the hotel they had a free lunch in the bar too. I got to admit I nibbled some at that while I played cards."

"You a poor liar," DeLuca said from his bed.

"What?"

He said something that Longarm did not quite catch, then had to repeat it in Italian for his pretty wife to translate.

"He says no free lunch in hotel bar."

Hell, the truth was that Longarm had not bothered to pay any attention when he was in there. But every damn place had a free lunch, didn't it?

"Special occasion, I guess, with all the extra people in town," he lied quickly. "They sure had one tonight." He smiled.

So did the DeLucas.

"You would like some tea?" Mrs. DeLuca offered.

95

"We have no coffee, but Grandma gathers herbs at their time for picking. Very good tea."

"Yes, ma'am, I'd like that."

She left the room again. DeLuca motioned Longarm to the only chair in the room.

Longarm sat and pulled out a cheroot. "Mind if I smoke?"

"'Salright. You smoke."

Longarm thought the man was looking rather longingly at the cigar. He brought out another and offered it to DeLuca.

"You sure?"

"Sure, I got plenty of them upstairs."

DeLuca accepted the slim cheroot with a smile of great pleasure, and Longarm lighted both of them.

"Ah," DeLuca said with satisfaction. He lay back against his pillows with the cheroot in one hand and the plate of ham and breadsticks close to the other. He looked thoroughly contented.

Mrs. DeLuca returned with a tray bearing three cups and a steaming pot. She poured the unsweetened tea for all three of them. She did not offer sugar, and Longarm assumed that they had none in the house.

"This is very good, ma'am." He did not have to lie about that. The tea was a weak, pale color, but the flavor was rich and quite pleasant, if very much different from anything he had had before.

She told him what the herbs were, but he had no idea if she was telling him in Italian or English.

"You are in the politics, Mr. Long?" she asked when the silence threatened to become strained.

"No, ma'am." There seemed no reason not to, so Longarm told them what he did.

Mrs. DeLuca accepted the information with polite interest. Her husband nodded and said something to her. Whatever it was, she scoffed at it and said something sharp back at him.

"What was that?" Longarm asked.

She waved a hand toward her obviously silly husband. "Him. He says it is like his papa said a long time ago. He says now you have come to do what his papa said the gover'ment would do. Bah! His papa was a foolish old man."

DeLuca could not speak all that much English, but apparently he could understand it just fine. He exploded into a loud outburst in Italian that, if it was not cussing, should have been. Mrs. DeLuca gave him as good as she was getting, and for a little while there it was downright noisy in the small room.

Longarm did not know whether he should try to slip quietly away or wait it out and pretend there was no argument taking place here. For the moment he settled for drinking his tea and trying to look invisible.

"You tell 'im," Mrs. DeLuca demanded, drawing a most unwilling visitor into the argument. "You tell this man, Marshal, that you don' come here to arrest that dam' Mr. Gort."

Longarm began to wish he could speak Italian. "Is there some reason Senator Gort should be arrested?" he asked.

DeLuca gave his wife a triumphantly malicious smile and nodded.

She ignored him and turned to Longarm. She shrugged. "Everybody knows Mr. Gort is a bad man, but everybody knows nobody ever gonna bring the law on him."

"You don't like him here?"

She pantomimed spitting on the floor. "No one likes that man here."

"But you keep electing him to the state senate," Longarm said.

"Everybody here also work for him, Marshal. It is his people who count the vote. Always the big vote, always the big numbers. But you don' see so many going to the courthouse that day. Pah!"

DeLuca said something and laughed. His wife grinned and leaned over to touch his wrist. As far as Longarm could tell, they might never have been fighting. She turned to Longarm and said, "He says besides, that's the best way to keep the old sumbitch away from here."

Longarm grinned at them both.

"But tell me," he said, "what is it that Gort is supposed to have done?"

He leaned forward and listened, the tea forgotten, while the two DeLucas told him what they knew and all that the community suspected.

Chapter 14

If there was a candle or a lamp in Longarm's room, he did not know where it was. Still deep in thought from the conversation he had just had, he left the door ajar to get the benefit of a candle left burning in the hallway—surely left there for his benefit, since he was certain the DeLuca family could not afford such a luxury as a matter of course—and groped around in the nearly dark room. He walked into a piece of furniture that had not been there when he last saw the room and knew that, in spite of his protests, they had moved a bed in for him.

Longarm heard a faint rustle of motion from the darkness, and without having to think about it the Colt Thunderer was in his palm and searching for possible danger.

There was a brittle, scratching noise and then the flare of a match.

Longarm's finger tightened slightly on the trigger

of the Colt, then relaxed when the flareup of the small but intense flame revealed the handsome features of the elder Mrs. DeLuca.

"You startled me, ma'am."

"So I see. You will not shoot me now?"

"No, ma'am."

The damn woman was in bed. Longarm looked around, wondering if he had blundered into the wrong room by mistake. He thought sure this was the one he had been given, but...

The burning match grew shorter, and she shook it out.

"I'm sorry, ma'am. I musta got the wrong turn somewhere. Or something." He started to back out of the room.

From the darkness he could hear a low chuckle. "You made no mistake, Mr. Long. Put out the candle, please, then come back an' close the door."

Longarm felt a twinge of nervousness. There was no doubting the woman's intentions now. But, damn it, she was a *grandmother*.

"Go," she commanded.

Longarm did as he was told. He went back out into the hallway and extinguished the candle that had been left aflame on a small stand by the head of the stairs. He felt his way back into his room, wondering how he could politely get out of this situation. After all, the woman was attractive enough and all that, but...

He shut the door behind him. The woman struck another match and leaned to the side to find and light an oil lamp sitting on another stand beside the bed.

The motion caused the bedsheet to fall away from her body. She was naked, and Longarm's breath caught in his throat. She might be old enough to be a grandmother, but she had a body to make a man's mouth water.

Her breasts were large and full. They drooped only slightly. Her hair, unpinned and brushed out loose and long, was as dark as coal and hung down across her shoulders to rest lightly on those full breasts. There was no gray in her hair. It was so glossy and gleaming it looked like it had been oiled.

She smiled at him and deliberately swept the sheet away.

The rest of her body met the promise of her breasts. Her belly was pale and creamy, her thighs firm and well proportioned. The vee of jet hair in her crotch held a promise of strength and greedy heat. There were a few, very few, silver hairs nested in that dark patch. Longarm felt a quick stir of response.

She must have noticed the rising interest, because her eyes drifted down below his belt, and she laughed with pleasure.

Longarm still had the Colt in his hand, forgotten there. He shoved it back into the cross-draw holster on his belly.

"One should think," she said, "that you would be used to visitors in the night, Mr. Long. You are a most handsome man."

Longarm cleared his throat. He was feeling awkward and, for some reason, a little shy here. It was the thought of her age that was putting him off, he knew. That and the thought that this definitely attractive woman was, for crying out loud, the mother of his host.

She dropped the spent match into a cracked saucer that had been put out for him to use as an ashtray, then left the bed, stepping aside so the lamplight fell on her and he could see all that she was offering.

She posed there for him for a moment, certain of her appeal, and when Longarm swallowed hard again once or twice she laughed and came toward him.

"Damn it, Mrs. DeLuca..." His throat felt dry, and he had a little trouble forming the words.

She stopped in front of him and began to help him off with his coat, his vest, the buckle of his belt.

Desire overcame his reluctance, and he reached for her.

She unbuttoned his shirt first and spread it wide before she came to him, then pressed the heat of her flesh against his chest. It was like she was taking a kind of satisfaction from the contact with his naked, hairy chest. She moaned softly when she touched him, and her hips wriggled insistently against him as she pressed that dark thatch of curly hair against the buttons of his fly.

She was a tall woman, only inches shorter than Longarm, and when he bent to her she kissed him with a fierce eagerness.

His tongue probed deep into her mouth, and she answered in kind.

Her fingers fluttered to his waist, swiftly working at the buttons of his trousers, and after a moment his britches slid to the floor.

Her hands continued to search, finding and then fondling him.

She gasped when she traced the long, hard length of him, then sighed with pleasure when she reached around and under to cup his balls in the palm of her hand.

"So long," she muttered against the press of his mouth. "It has been so very long."

Longarm kicked free of his fallen trousers but did

not want to take the time to bend down and remove his boots.

He walked her backward and lowered her onto the waiting bed.

There would be time enough for fancy work later. Right now he only wanted to socket himself deep inside this woman's body.

She opened herself to him and pulled him down on top of her. She was damply warm and ready to receive him.

He plunged into her, her hands guiding him and pulling him closer.

Her hips arched up to meet him, and her legs, long and strong, wrapped around him to clasp and hold him within her.

She nuzzled into the hollow of his throat, and her breath was as hot as her sex. Her hips began to pump and to pull, eager to drain him and take his seed into herself.

Longarm held back, allowing her time to build her responses, but he did not need to hold himself in check for long. Within moments her breath was rasping in her throat and her movements became frantic.

Longarm let go then, ramming and bucking into her flesh, driving himself faster and deeper into her. And she gave back as good as she got, lifting her hips to meet his every stroke with a rising, thrashing frenzy that ended in a shuddering climax of pent-up needs finding release.

She collapsed under him, her weight dropping dead against the yielding bed and her arms and legs falling away from him. Her breath came in short, gasping spurts, and she was smiling.

Longarm drew back from her slightly and smiled down at her.

She looked puzzled. She wriggled her hips exper-
imentally, then asked, "You did not?"

He smiled again. "Not yet." He bent to kiss her.
"We got time. Lots of time."

She sighed, and her arms wrapped happily around
him again. "Yes. We have very much time now." She
reached under his sweat-slicked belly and shifted her
position so she could reach around him where he was
still plunged hard and deep inside her and toyed lightly
with the heavy sack of his scrotum.

"So much time," she murmured.

She lay very still, her hips not moving at all, yet
Longarm could feel a slow, soft beginning of gentle
contractions inside her as she began to stroke and to
milk him with internal muscles that he had not suspected.

He grinned his appreciation of the control, and she
smiled back at him.

The grin became a laugh and he said, "You know,
that there would make a hell of a parlor trick. But I
just don't know how you could show it off in the
parlor."

She chuckled and speeded up the rhythm of the
rippling pull, still without moving her hips or pelvis.

What the hell, Longarm thought. He would just
have to be polite and go along with the program here.

He let her have her fun, and it no longer seemed
to matter a lick that she was the mother of a grown
man or that she had a passel of grandchildren sleeping
not far off in this same house somewhere.

Chapter 15

"You are a very late sleeping man, Marshal," the younger Mrs. DeLuca said when he finally came downstairs.

"Yes, ma'am. Well, I had some trouble getting to sleep last night. I reckon that's what put me off schedule."

The older Mrs. DeLuca was busy washing dishes on the far side of the kitchen. She did not look in his direction or in any way acknowledge the hours they had spent together while Longarm was having that difficulty falling asleep.

Lordy, he thought. He had no idea what the woman's name was. He had to stifle a grin, hiding the expression from the woman's daughter-in-law, when he realized he could not exactly call her Grandma DeLuca if she should happen to want a repeat performance in the near future.

"We had ham and eggs for the morning meal," the younger woman was saying. "Thanks to you. We have saved you some for your meal."

"No, thanks, ma'am. I hardly ever want anything to eat when I first get up," he lied. That food could be better served into the stomachs of those children, he figured. He could go over to the hotel for his breakfast.

"As you wish," she said, giving him no argument about it. "You can be here tonight for the gathering you wish?"

"Yes, ma'am." Last night the DeLucas had promised to bring in a bunch of other Italian quarry workers and, possibly more important, servants from the Gort household to talk with him in private.

"The children have gone to tell them," the younger Mrs. DeLuca said. "Eight o'clock?"

"That would be just fine, ma'am. I appreciate all you and the mister are doing to help me."

She shrugged.

"I'll fetch back something to feed them all," he said.

She smiled. "It will be as a party. We have not had a party in very much time."

"Then I reckon it's time you did." He glanced past the young wife and mother. The older Mrs. DeLuca still had not so much as turned around from her dish-washing chores to acknowledge his existence this morning.

But that was all right. She damn sure had done more than that during the night. Quite frankly, Long-arm was hoping she would want to do it all over again tonight after the company had gone.

Just thinking about that gave him a quick surge of

106

interest, and he had to turn away to keep the woman's daughter-in-law from seeing the sudden bulge of his britches.

He left the house and hiked back up the hill to the business district. It was Saturday morning, and apparently many of the well-heeled politicians who had come to express their support for Hiram Gort's candidacy had also slept in late this morning. The hotel restaurant was crowded and noisy. Longarm looked in on the confusion but decided he did not want to join it. He went back out onto the sidewalk and searched the signs up and down the short business district for a cafe.

There was one other halfway decent-looking eatery in Brownstone, but it too was uncomfortably full and just as loud as the hotel restaurant had been. Longarm ambled on down the dusty street in search of a meal.

He finally found a greasy-looking place that obviously catered to the working-class men, probably quarrymen and stonecutters without wives to cook for them. At this time of day, even on a holiday weekend, the place was deserted. Longarm went inside and took a seat at the window end of the one long table that served all of the cafe's customers.

He ordered the best the place had to offer and, while he waited, gazed out the window at the masses of people beginning to surge up and down the street.

Nearly all of them, men and women alike, were very well dressed. They gave the drab little town a busy, festive air that it undoubtedly lacked throughout the rest of the year.

Longarm could not help but wonder how many of these people were genuinely in support of Hiram Cort for the governor's race, how many of them were merely here to see and be seen, to build bridges toward the seat of power just in case Gort should happen to gain election.

That was something that always troubled Longarm about these political types. A man never knew when they were offering something genuine or when they were simply covering their own asses.

He shook his head. In many ways he felt more comfortable about the workers who, unseen among the crowd, like so many lampposts or docile draft animals, were engaged in the stringing of banners and pennants and bunting along the storefronts and across the street.

These men working with hammers and ladders to prepare the town for the festivities to come wore rough clothing and rundown shoes that were colorless from the application of years of rock dust. They worked with the sleeves of their shirts rolled up over powerful forearms and thick wrists, and they worked bareheaded in the bright sunshine. The hammers looked small in their hands. Quarrymen, Longarm thought, taken away from their usual jobs to perform this service for the man who controlled their lives as well as their jobs.

At least that was the way the DeLucas had represented Brownstone's situation to him last night. He reminded himself that whatever they said should be examined closely, because DeLuca had an admitted grudge against Hiram Gort. Anything the man said about Gort would have to be considered in that light.

Longarm's meal came. It was palatable, but barely so. He ate it quickly, with no particular enjoyment, and left the cafe without hanging around for the extra cups of coffee that he usually enjoyed after breakfast.

At least the meal had been cheap.

He paused outside on the narrow stoop in front of the cafe to light a cheroot. He cupped his hands around the flare of the match and bent his head to it.

"G'mornin', Mister Marshal."

Longarm shook the match out and squinted up past a rising curl of smoke to look at the man who had spoken. He was one of the workmen, dark-haired and olive-complected like so many in the town, who was tacking bunting along the front of the cafe.

"Good morning."

The man gave him a cheerful flash of white teeth and went back to his work. Longarm wandered on without particular purpose for the moment. There was little he could do now until this evening, when he would meet with the people the DeLucas were assembling for him.

It was obvious that the word was already spreading through the Italian community here. The man who had spoken to him had called him marshal, but Longarm's badge was in his wallet, tucked away in a coat pocket.

He did not really want to mingle with the self-important swells in town, so he idled off in the other direction.

He passed a platform that was in the last stages of construction. It was obviously a speaking platform, probably where Gort and his supporters would deliver the patriotic and political addresses that would fill the weekend.

A swarm of workmen were already hanging red, white, and blue bunting around the rails and draping the front of the large podium with more of the distinctive coloring while carpenters finished laying the flooring where the mighty would sit.

The stage was placed at the edge of the town, facing a large, open lot overgrown with weeds but completely—and, Longarm suspected, recently—cleared of any trash or litter.

A wagon pulled to a halt in front of the platform, and a group of dark-haired teenage boys piled out of it to begin unloading and setting up lines of chairs where the guests would sit facing the speakers.

Could all of this, Longarm wondered, have come from a start provided by Pop Sweeley's murderous gang?

It was sad but true, he decided, that the possibility was strong enough that it at least had to be investigated.

Sweeley, as close as they had been able to figure back then, must have taken in an awful lot of cash while he was in business. Damn little had ever been recovered. The missing loot had to have gone somewhere. Maybe into Hiram Gort's pockets.

Longarm strolled on. He finished his cheroot and flicked it into the road he was following. The road looked like it ended about fifty yards farther on, although that made no sense.

A few more long paces and Longarm could see he had been wrong. The road did not end; it dropped off into a steep decline.

As he reached the lip of the dropoff, Longarm could see that the road had been cut into virtually solid rock here in a series of switchbacks down a cliff face.

He stood at the top of the cliff and looked down into the deep quarry that was Brownstone's reason for being.

The drop from where he stood was several hundred

sheer feet. Probably at one time there had been an upjutting formation of the red stone here, but years of cutting and quarrying had reduced the original formations, and now the workmen were having to haul the rock up from a laboriously manmade pit to reach the rail line. Before the coming of the railroad, Longarm thought, it must have been hell trying to freight the rock out to where it could be sold.

A strong wind came up at Longarm's back, and he had to brace himself against it. He took a careful step backward away from the edge of the quarried cliff. One misstep here, and a man would fall to certain death on the hard red stone far below.

He pulled another cheroot from his pocket, bit off the twisted tobacco at the tip, and spat it out. As he pulled out a match, he dropped the damn cheroot onto the stony, nearly bare soil at the lip of the cliff.

Shit, he told himself. He bent to pick up the cigar.

As he did so he heard the angry, quick sizzle of a large-caliber slug passing just overhead . . . just where his head had been a moment before.

It was several heartbeats later before he heard the hollow, distinctive report of the muzzle blast from a heavy rifle.

By that time Custis Long was already sprawled face down on the ground with his Colt in his hand but with no damned idea of where his target might be.

Longarm stood and brushed the dust from his coat and trousers. The Colt was still in his hand, though, and his eyes were busy searching the area back toward Brownstone. It was from somewhere in that direction that the shot had been fired, but he still had no idea

111

of exactly where the rifleman had been. It had been fifteen minutes or longer, and he had seen no hint of motion, no puff of powder smoke, nothing.

Standing, he was able to see now that the work on the speaking platform had been finished. The chairs were all set out and the workmen gone.

Beyond the platform he could see a few small boys playing behind the nearest of the town buildings. One of them threw something, and a moment later there was a flash of brightness on the ground, followed shortly by the sharp report of a firecracker going off.

Damn, Longarm thought. If anyone had heard the gunshot they would only have thought it a firecracker and probably paid no attention. Likely it would do no good to ask if anyone had seen or heard anything.

He stood for a while, still alert and watchful, and tried to remember exactly where the shot would have come from. As nearly as he could figure, it must have been from somewhere in the vicinity of the piles of quarried and shaped rock, stacked near the rails ready for shipment.

It was a logical place, he thought. Close enough to the business section for the gunman to have faded into the crowd afterward but isolated enough, with no reason for anyone to be hanging around among the stacks of stone, to give the man privacy.

He wanted to know where the shot had been fired from. But more than that, Longarm wanted to know who had fired it. And why.

After a time he shoved the Colt back into his holster—not that a handgun would do much good at the distances to the nearest cover anyway—and walked toward the piles of shaped stone.

He counted his paces while he went, stretching

each step beyond the standard thirty-inch pace to an approximate yard. He grunted when he reached the closest pile of stone veneer. Three hundred thirty-six yards. That was a hell of a shot by anybody's standards. If, that is, he was correct in assuming that this was where the shot would have been fired.

He looked around, but there was no empty cartridge case on the ground. Nothing to tell him if he was right.

The gritty, dust-coated soil was foot-tracked all through the piles of stone, so he could not tell anything from that. Not without having had the foresight to inspect the ground for tracks beforehand. And beforehand there had been no indication that he would have to think about such a thing.

He grunted to himself and pulled another cheroot from his pocket. The one he had prepared to light earlier was still on the ground out by the edge of the quarry cliff.

He lit his cigar and poked around some more. There was a place on top of one pile of stone, almost head-high, where the dust seemed to have been disturbed. It *could* have been done by a man who rested a rifle and forearm on top of the rock to steady his aim for the long shot.

On the other hand, it could have been done by a bird, a kid, by nearly any damn thing. There was just no way he could tell.

He looked around. From here the town buildings and the railroad station were hidden from view by other, taller stacks of red stone. That proved nothing except that he was unlikely to locate any witnesses.

"Bitch," he mumbled out loud.

Who fired the shot? Why?

He had no answers, nor any reasonable expectation of finding any. Not without more information.

"Bitch," he said again.

He walked back into Brownstone and joined the throngs of people who were milling in the street.

It was nearing noon now, and people were beginning to drift down toward the platform at the edge of the town.

Longarm joined the flow of people.

"The *signore* is our *patrone*," the old man was saying. "He is *good* man. Provides for our jobs. Yes. It was the *signore* who brought the railroad to us. The jobs, they were poor before the railroad came. Very few men needed. Very few jobs. Very hard to ship the stone we cut. It was the *signore* with his railroad who change all this. Many jobs now. Much better. You ask. They will tell you."

The old man, who seemed to be the patriarch of the Italian community in Brownstone, had been saying very much the same thing for the past half-hour. During that time he had not given Longarm a chance to ask anything of the other people who were gathered in the DeLucas' stuffy little parlor.

Longarm had been introduced to him, but had been unable to make any sense out of the swift roll of sounds that were his name. Apparently the old man had had to be included, as a matter of local protocol. Longarm understood that without being particularly appreciative of the necessity. He suspected the evening would have been much more productive without the old fossil trying to run the show as a gathering in praise of Senator Hiram Gort, which was obviously the old

114

fellow's intention. The old man sounded like a mechanical parrot, repeating the same thing over and over again, giving no one else a chance to get a word in edgewise.

Longarm waited him out patiently and ignored the agreement that the others muttered from time to time. Eventually the old man ran out of wind. He set his coffee cup aside—the beans provided by Longarm, along with an assortment of goodies for the DeLucas to serve—and stood. He leaned on his cane and glared around the room at the others, then bowed with stiff formality toward Longarm and, without another word, left the house. Little Tony DeLuca grabbed up a lantern and followed the old man out to light his way home. Longarm hoped that this was not all he was going to hear tonight.

With the old man gone, there was a lessening of tension in the room. Until it disappeared, Longarm had not really been aware of the stiffness with which the others held themselves. Now they all seemed to relax.

The younger Mrs. DeLuca smiled. "Signore Gionanno likes you," she said. "He could have told everyone to go home."

"Would they have done it?"

"Of course." She acted like he was slightly daft for having asked such a foolish question.

"Then I'm glad he liked me." But damned if he had been able to tell that, Longarm thought to himself. He had not thought the old fart was thinking about anything except what a swell fellow Hiram Gort was.

"You must undersand," Mrs. DeLuca said, "it is necessary for him to speak as he docs. It means," she

115

shrugged, "no more than the words you listen to this afternoon when the speeches are made. You understand this?"

Maybe he did, Longarm decided. He nodded.

"Now." She turned toward a plump, matronly woman Longarm recognized from having seen her working in Gort's kitchen the night before. "Anna?"

The woman said something at length in Italian. When she stopped, it was not Mrs. DeLuca who offered Longarm the translation, but a middle-aged, very handsome man whose upper arms threatened to burst through the seams of his shirt.

"Mrs. Carano has worked in the *patrone's* house since the time of the young *signorina*," he said. "She was nurse to the *signorina*, then maid when the child became the bride of the *patrone*. You know what I am saying to you?"

"I don't think so," Longarm admitted.

The man—Longarm thought his name was Adamo, but whether that was his first name or last Longarm had not been able to guess—turned and said something to Anna.

She fumbled in a worn and discolored handbag for a moment and pulled out a fading daguerreotype that she handed to Longarm.

"*Signorina* Judith," she said with a motherly pride and affection.

Longarm looked at the severe young woman in the old picture. She was a girl, really. Probably in her mid- to late teens, and at the height of her natural beauty. Or should have been. The poor thing had had damn little to be proud of in that regard. She was a homely girl with bad teeth and a muddied complexion that even the poor quality of a daguerreotype could not hide. Her hair was thin and mousy and had been pulled back into a bun tight enough to draw at the corners of her eyes when she posed for the picture. Longarm looked at her and turned the metal plate over in his hands, but there was no date engraved on it. It looked old.

"Who is she?" he asked.

"Was," Adamo corrected.

"Oh?"

"She was the *Signorina* Judith Brown. It was her father, who once was the *patrone*, Charles Brown, who started the quarry an' brought us here to make our living with the stone we knew in the old country."

"Yes?"

"It was the *signore*, now the *patrone*, who came here later. Long time ago now, but before the railroad. He married the *signorina*. Very fast. Anna says the *signorina* carried his child. Before the wedding. You know?"

Longarm shrugged, but privately he agreed that a man would have to be pretty hard up to voluntarily hitch up with a girl that ugly.

"Very fast wedding, yes," Adamo said. "The old *patrone*, he died soon. Got very sick and died soon. A month, no more, after the wedding. The young *signora* was very unhappy. She went for long walks in the night then. One night she walked out on the cliff. The new *patrone*, he waited for her. When she did not come in, he woke the people in the house. Had them go look for her. We found her in the morning, all broken on the rocks. The *patrone*, he did not cry."

Anna interrupted with an outburst of impassioned Italian, and Adamo said, "Anna knows the *patrone* pushed her from the cliff. He killed her to gain the quarry of her dead papa. She *knows* this to be true."

"How would she know that?" Longarm asked.

Adamo turned and asked Anna something, then turned back to Longarm and said, "The *patrone* had dust on his shoes. She saw it in the morning."

"So?"

"When the *patrone* came here he had old boots. Soon as he married the *signorina* he threw the boots away and wore nothing but fine shoes. Anna's eldest boy, he had to polish the shoes each night. The *patrone* wore nothing but fine shoes after that. Today he wears nothing but fine shoes polished every night."

"Couldn't he have looked for the girl himself, before he woke everyone to help?" Longarm asked.

Adamo shrugged.

Anna spat out something that sounded like cussing, even though Longarm did not know a word of Italian.

"What about the rest of you?" Longarm asked. "Does anyone else know anything about the senator?"

He listened, but all they had to offer was a collection of speculation and rumor. He was polite about it. He listened attentively to everything he was told.

But the truth was, there was damn little to hear. Business deals rejected at one meal, shakily accepted at the next. Rumors of buyers who left without buying stone from the quarry and never returned.

None of it, Longarm knew, added up to a damn thing of real interest.

Not even, really, the plump woman's assertions about Judith Brown Gort and her death.

There just was not anything here to hang a case on.

And, damn it, all of what there was indicated that

118

Gort had come here without anything in his pockets and gained what he could by marrying Charles Brown's daughter.

If Longarm accepted every word these people were telling him, accepted it all as gospel, it still left Sweeley and his thugs completely out of the picture.

"Do any of you know anything about a man named Sweeley?" Longarm asked. "Anything at all?"

They spoke among themselves, then Adamo shook his head.

Longarm described Sweeley for them. None of them remembered seeing or hearing anything about a man like that.

Longarm sighed. It looked, he thought, like a dead issue.

He thanked them for their help—although they had given him none—and the gathering turned into a party, these local working people having their own kind of Fourth festivities with the food and drink Longarm had provided.

That, at least, was worth the doing, he thought. The DeLucas seemed to be thoroughly enjoying themselves. He was glad about that.

Chapter 16

She came into the room shortly after the party broke up and the visitors went home. It was not late. Working people, even on a holiday weekend, had to get to bed early if they expected to get to work early the following morning.

Longarm was already in bed, but he had left the lamp burning in anticipation. He smiled when she opened the door and slipped inside.

She was still wearing the housedress she had had on all day. It was plain, even drab, but the fullness of her figure was too fine to be hidden.

She smiled back at him and raised a finger to her lips to ask for silence. She pointed down the hallway toward where the children would be sleeping, and he understood. Some of the kids must not yet be asleep. She had not spoken half a dozen words to him, Longarm realized, all day long. Yet obviously her nocturnal interests were quite as strong as they had been before.

Still without speaking, Grandma DeLuca—*damn*, he told himself, he was going to *have* to learn her name tonight—began to strip quickly out of the many layers of clothing society demanded she wear.

One piece after another, the dress and the undergarments were thrown into a heap on the floor, and her smile became broader as each one was discarded. She turned her back at one point and let Longarm help her out of what he considered to be a totally unnecessary corset. She turned back to face him before she stripped her chemise over her head, exposing large breasts veined faintly blue just beneath the surface of her flesh.

She stepped out of her drawers and kicked them aside, then took a step backward and posed there for him to see.

Her body was positively magnificent, built for use, and her expression was one of pleasure and pride as he looked at her. Her nipples were already engorged and standing proudly erect.

Longarm beckoned her close, and she came to him. He leaned forward to take first one nipple and then the other into his mouth, rolling them from side to side with his tongue and sucking gently on them.

The woman stroked his head, smoothing the hair back from his forehead and running her hands over the planes of hard muscle on his shoulders and back. She moaned softly.

Still without speaking, she pulled away from him and placed her fingertips on his chest, pushing him back slightly into a sitting position on the side of the bed.

She knelt on the hardwood floor in front of him

and levered his knees wide. She used her hands to toy with him first, admiringly tracing the length of him with her fingers. Then she bent and pressed the head of his cock against the softness of her cheek. He could feel the warmth of her breath as she turned her head and lightly kissed him up and down his shaft. With her other hand she cupped his balls, obviously enjoying the rich, full weight of them. Her head dipped lower, and she began to lick his balls. Then higher, her tongue moving slowly and delicately, without hurry.

She pulled the foreskin back to expose the bulbous red head and encircled it with her tongue and then with her lips.

"You don't have to do that," he whispered.

She stopped what she was doing and looked up at him. "Do you know how many years it is since I have had the taste of a man on my tongue?"

The question did not require an answer. He let her do as she wished.

She bent to him again, this time taking him deep into her mouth. She was not young, but she seemed not to be greatly experienced at this. What she lacked in experience, though, she more than made up in willingness. She sucked at him with a genuine desire that stirred him more than any professional expertise could have, and within moments Longarm could feel the urgent responses deep within his groin. He could feel the rising flood of hot release, and he made no effort to hold it back. He held himself very still, not wanting to choke her, and let her pull the sweet, hot flow from him. She was the one who moaned as the overheated juices spurted and flowed into her mouth.

Still she stayed with him, continuing to suck as if asking for more, and he clenched his fists and pressed them against the sheets, but managed to hold himself rigid and motionless as she drew the last of his sperm into herself.

She gulped and swallowed and almost choked herself once, but she remained with him until the final drop was spent. Only then did she release him, still stroking him gently with her fingertips, and rock back onto her heels.

She looked pleased, proud of herself. She smiled up at him and he bent forward to stroke her cheek and smooth the long spill of black hair that framed her face.

She sighed.

Longarm crooked a finger, and she came forward to join him on the bed.

He wrapped his arms around her, and they lay for a while pressed together with her breasts warm against his chest and her breath coming slow and relaxed into the hollow of his throat.

"Lovely," he whispered.

"Yes."

Her needs had not yet been met, but there was time. They lay cuddled quietly together for some time until Longarm felt the return of desire and rolled her onto her back.

Her expression when he leaned over her to kiss her and cup her breasts was one of gratitude as well as desire.

He raised himself over her, and she opened herself to him, reached down to find and to guide him.

She was drippingly wet and more than ready, and when he entered her he found her to be tighter than any woman this age had a right to be. He had not noticed that the night before, in the heat of their passion, but this time the pace was slower and the sensations deeper and more gentle. He could not help but wonder just how long it had been since she had been with a man, but it was not the sort of thing he could ask.

He slid into her slowly, giving her time to adjust to his size, easing forward and then back, then again a little deeper as the penetration increased. She lay compliant beneath him and let him dictate the pace of the joining until finally he was socketed fully within her.

Her body remained still, but by then her breath was catching in her throat and she rolled her head from side to side.

Longarm let his weight down onto her until she bore all of it over her pelvic structure. He lay on top of her, quiet and still fully inside her, and turned her face toward him so he could kiss her.

She groaned softly, and her needs took over control of her body. Her hips began to writhe and pump in slow, involuntary spurts as she sought to take more and more into herself. He could feel the hard ridge of bone structure beneath the softness of her belly as she raised herself to him.

Longarm raised himself slightly and braced into a rigid position just inches above her, with nearly all of his shaft still inside her.

She responded as he knew she would, raising herself to him and then dropping her body away, setting the pace herself now, as he remained immobile above her.

Her breathing was coming harsh and ragged in her throat, and the speed of her hip movements increased.

Longarm could feel her tighten, and her arms crept

around to encircle and clutch at him.

He could feel the stiffening shudders when her release came. She bit her lip to keep herself from crying out, and he was reminded that her grandchildren were just down the hall in another bedroom. That flavor of furtivenes added to the pleasure somehow, and he had to steel himself to keep from joining her in her climax, although he had not thought he was anywhere near a climax of his own.

She shuddered and shook and choked back her cries of pleasure, and when she was done her expression was one of raw, sheer joy.

He lay on top of her again and gave her time to recover, then—very slowly at first—began once again to stroke deep into her and withdraw until he was poised at the outer lips of her black-furred sex.

He concentrated on her responses and gave her time to rise to meet him, and when finally he plunged deep into her for the final time, his release was matched with a convulsive clenching of her arms and her thighs fiercely tight around him.

Drained, utterly spent at least for the moment, he rolled away from her and let her nestle contentedly against his side.

Longarm woke realizing that he must have dozed, at least for a few minutes. He was slightly disoriented and unsure of the passage of time, although he believed it had not been great. The woman was still awake at his side, waiting patiently for him to return to her. She smiled when she saw his eyes flutter open. She reached for him, fondling him with pleasure.

There was something, though . . .

There was something out of place. Something,

whatever it was, that had wakened him.

He ignored her seeking hand and rolled aside, rising to his feet beside the bed in a swift, fluid motion.

His hand swept automatically for the holstered Colt hanging at the head of the bed, and he looked around the room.

The lamp still burned as it had before. Nothing was out of place. He knew with complete certainty that the woman had not left the bed while he slept. Her motion would have wakened him if she had.

Whatever it was that had brought him out of his sleep, it had been nothing in this room.

With the Colt in his hand, he went to the window and pulled the flour-sack drape a few inches aside.

He could see nothing in the darkness out there. He turned and blew out the lamp, gave his eyes a moment to adjust, and returned to the window.

There was a hint of movement in the shadows below him. Directly below the window, and almost beyond his line of sight from the second-story window.

There was that flicker of shadowy motion and then the sound of something splashing. Something liquid.

He blinked. He felt slightly fuzzy from the interrupted slumber. He knew he should be able to make some sense out of this, but at the moment he could not. He blinked again.

Light flared, yellow and startlingly bright, and then he knew what it was.

Someone down there had just struck a match.

"Fire!" Longarm yelled into the night.

He leaned forward, out of the window, bringing the .44 Colt to bear just as the son of a bitch down below tossed the match.

126

Coal oil—he could smell it now—caught and flamed, the heat rising swiftly to batter Longarm's face.

The rush of the flame was frighteningly swift, and he could feel it sear his moustache and eyebrows within the span of a heartbeat.

The arsonist was clearly caught in the light of the quick flames, and Longarm triggered a shot down at him.

He had time to see the man's left leg buckle from the impact of the heavy slug. Then the crackling gout of oil-fired flame drove him back inside the window.

Flame licked hungrily at the sacking hung across the open window. Longarm snatched the glazed sash down so hard the glass shattered.

Son of a *bitch*, he told himself. That was not doing any good.

He tried to lean out of the broken window again to get another shot at the man who had set the fire, but the flames were too high now.

He grabbed the drapes from the window and yanked them down. Having given the fire access to the room, he did not want to give it any more to feed on than was necessary. At least the damn house was built of stone. Only the framing of the doors and windows would be vulnerable to fire.

He turned toward the woman, but she was already gone. Her dress was missing, but all of her other things remained tumbled on the foor.

Longarm realized that the door to the hallway was standing open, and he was standing there with his bare ass hanging out.

Elsewhere in the house, he could hear shouts of

alarm. The children were crying, and Mrs. DeLuca was calming them, giving them gentle but firm instructions in Italian.

Longarm grabbed his clothing and his gear. He pulled his clothes on and threw his carpetbag and saddle as far out the window as he could heave them. He had no time to carry them out now. He had to go help make sure the children and the bedridden DeLuca were safe.

Chapter 17

Longarm helped the young Mrs. DeLuca carry her husband outside. He found the two of them struggling in the hall downstairs, grabbed up the wasted young man, and ran out into the cool night with him.

Grandma DeLuca—why, oh *why,* damn it, hadn't he asked her name when he had the chance?—was right behind them with the last of the children.

Longarm took a quick head count to make sure all of the children were safe, then raced around to the back of the house.

Neighbors were already streaming in to help, buckets and pails and shovels in their hands. The alarm had spread quickly.

With that much help at hand, Longarm thought the damage to the house should be minimal. Now he wanted to find the man who had been unfeeling enough to set fire to a house full of children.

That son of a bitch Longarm wanted. Bad.

He swung wide to stay out of the circle of light from the already diminishing flames at the back of the house.

Neighbors who were chattering wildly in Italian were already there, beating the fire into submission with water and blankets. But there was no sign on the ground of the man who had set the fire.

Longarm was sure he had hit the man. The shot had been true. He had seen the man's leg go out from under him.

The bastard must have crawled away. He could not have gone far.

The .44 held ready in his hand, Longarm ghosted silently through the darkness.

He circled about seventy yards out from the house, moving cautiously, knowing there might be a bullet spitting death at him from any shadow.

He cursed the necessity for moving so slowly, but he had no choice about it. Not if he wanted to remain alive.

A sound reached him, cutting through the distant shouts of the helping neighbors. It came from somewhere to his right, the soft, metallic snick of a hammer being drawn back to a cocked position.

Longarm dropped to the ground, bruising his ribs on chunks of rock, but intent on getting the hell out of the way.

A lance of yellow flame speared the night, pointed toward the place where he had just been, and the thunderclap of a gunshot followed immediately behind.

There. Beside that boulder.

The light was impossibly poor, but Longarm could

130

make out a black shape against the faintly lighter black of the night.

He could see nothing of the man who had shot at him, but he could make out where the bastard had to be hiding.

Longarm triggered the Colt, then again, and twin flashes of shockingly bright flame illuminated the ground in front of him.

Longarm rolled swiftly aside and came to rest several yards away with his revolver leveled toward the place where he had seen the gunfire.

A second shot came from the place immediately beside the low boulder. It hit the ground where Longarm had just been. He could hear the rattle of thrown gravel falling to earth yards beyond the point of impact.

Longarm bobbed to his knees and again fired twice into the shadows, aiming low. He fired and threw himself sideways, rolling once again and coming into a prone position with the Colt held at the ready.

This time there was no answering fire.

Longarm was too old a hand at this game to be taken in by a possum ruse.

He had time. And time was more valuable than blood. If the son of a bitch was already dead, he would keep where he was. If he was alive, Longarm would give him all the time he wanted to panic or to try to get away. From where he lay, Longarm would be able to hear any movement the man made on the gravel. He could not run. He certainly could not crawl away without Longarm knowing he was alive and moving.

Longarm stretched out flat on the ground and rested his cheek against his arm. He turned his head silently to look back toward the house.

The quickly assembled bucket brigade seemed to have the fire completely under control now. Even the shouting had died down, to be replaced with low voices filled with concern and sympathy.

With any luck, Longarm thought, the damage would not be severe. DeLuca probably would not be able to make repairs himself, but the family obviously had a great many friends in the area. They should be all right, he hoped.

He could not avoid, though, the nagging thought that it was his presence that had brought this trouble on them.

Someone had tried to shoot him earlier in the day. Now someone—the same person?—had tried to burn the DeLuca house with him sleeping inside it. The connection was too obvious to miss. It was his damned fault that the house had been fired.

He lay there, thinking sourly about things like that, but his ears tuned toward the deep shadows around the boulder not twenty yards away.

After half an hour, or possibly more, he heard a faint, rapid tattoo beat against the ground.

He thought he knew what it was.

It sounded like the final, convulsive jerkings of a man in the throes of death.

But that too could be faked. Longarm lay quiet and motionless where he was. He would have enjoyed a cheroot. At the moment he would have enjoyed even more a healthy slug of Maryland rye. Both of those could wait.

The first blush of dawn found Longarm awake and alert and still lying where he had been through what had been left of the night.

The DeLucas and their neighbors had long since returned to their beds. No one had bothered to look for him when they did. Probably they had forgotten all about him in their excitement.

Longarm stretched. His muscles were stiff and cramped after so many hours. At least in this dry climate there had been no dew to chill him. That was some measure of comfort.

He squinted into the growing light. There was little enough of it, a graying more than real light, but it was enough to let Longarm make out the hard outline of the boulder and beside it a formless mass that might have been another boulder or might as easily be the shape of a crumpled body.

He waited some more.

When he could see the red of a man's shirt he wiped the palm of his hand on his trouser leg and took a fresh grip on the Colt. He had long since had time to reload the .44.

He sat up.

There was no movement from the man on the ground. Longarm allowed himself a small measure of relaxation from the tension that had held him through the night.

He stood, aware of the stiffness in his joints, ready to snap a shot at the still figure if he saw any motion whatsoever.

He stood where he was for a moment, Colt already aimed, and allowed himself the sheer relief of a few shallow knee-bends to loosen his cramped muscles. Then he took a step forward, and another.

He saw a small, fluttering movement, and he had already fired into the silent body before he realized that a slight breeze had sprung up and the motion was only the fluttering of a dead man's hair.

Longarm's bullet struck its mark, square into the man's chest. The only result was the ugly, moist slap of sound at the impact. The body did not move at all.

Longarm reloaded the Colt from the loose rounds in his pocket and tried to holster it. It was only then that he realized that his holster was still back inside the house. He shoved the revolver into his hip pocket and went forward to examine the man he had killed.

He rubbed his eyes and smoothed his moustache down. He felt grainy and tired and more than a little irritable.

Behind him he could hear people stirring, probably brought out of their beds by the sound of his unnecessary gunshot.

"Shit," he muttered.

Chapter 18

No one seemed to know who the dead man was, which was surprising enough in a town the size of Brownstone. But what really amazed Longarm was that the man had not been armed when he came to burn the DeLuca house.

The rifle Longarm found at his side was Longarm's own Winchester lever gun. Apparently the fellow had found Longarm's saddle, with the scabbarded Winchester attached, when he was crawling away from the house. It was that weapon that he had used to shoot at the deputy afterward.

An examination of the corpse conducted in the Brownstone town marshal's office showed that he had been struck by only one bullet, obviously by Longarm's first shot through the house window. His upper thigh had been shattered by that slug and a number of minor arteries or veins severed. He eventually bled to death from the effects of that wound and was un-touched except for that, barring the bullet Longarm had put into his chest at dawn.

He carried no identification, and the only things Longarm found in his pockets were a rather dull clasp knife, two partial blocks of sulphur matches, a soiled handkerchief . . . and five twenty-dollar double eagles that were shiny new and unworn from use.

"He was paid to do that job," Longarm said, stab-bing with his forefinger at the double eagles lying bright yellow and gleaming on the town marshal's desk.

"If you say so." The marshal, a man by the name of Wilbertson, seemed unimpressed. He yawned and made no attempt to hide it. It was already long since clear that he did not appreciate being disturbed by some damned federal man early on a Sunday morning.

"And you say you don't know him?"

"Already told you that once," Wilbertson said. He yawned again, and pulled a cheap watch from his vest pocket. His meaning was obvious. Longarm ignored it.

"When will your undertaker get here?" he asked.

"Prob'ly," the marshal said, "when he's good an' woke up and has got a hot breakfast under his belt."

Sometimes, Longarm reflected, you found a local peace officer who was dedicated to his work, who cared about the welfare of the people he served, who would go out of his way to cooperate with anyone who could help assure the safety and welfare of his district's public. Then, on the other hand, there were knotheads like this Wilbertson.

Longarm looked at the corpse again. The body was temporarily laid out on a bench, thus occupying all of the available sitting space in the small office except for the marshal's own desk chair.

"We haven't stripped him," Longarm observed.

"Searched him," Wilbertson grunted. "Jonathan will do the rest."

Jonathan, Longarm assumed, would be the undertaker.

"I think I'll take a look," Longarm said. "Maybe he was carrying something else."

"Searched him already," the marshal said. He pulled a bandanna from his hip pocket and blew his nose loudly. He put the cloth away and from the same pocket pulled out a plug of tobacco and bit off a chew. At least, Longarm thought, the slob did not offer any to his visitor. Longarm lit a cheroot without offering one to Wilbertson.

That was another thing that pissed him off this morning, he thought. It turned out that when he threw his carpetbag out to safety, he had smashed his traveling bottle of rye. Now the bag and everything it contained reeked of rye whiskey. And, worse, until he could find time to get over to the hotel saloon, Longarm had none to drink. He could have enjoyed a shot about now.

Longarm ignored the local lawman and struggled by himself to pull the clothing off the dead man. It was not something that was easily done by one man.

The shirt was the worst, trying to work the arms out through the sleeves. Longarm was peeved enough and tired enough and irritable enough that he finally said the hell with it and cut the damn thing off.

The bullethole, a bloodless puncture since it had occurred long after the man's death by slow bleeding, he had already seen. He heaved the body onto its side.

"Say now," he mused out loud.

"Uh?"

"This man's got a tattoo on his right shoulder."

"So?"

"So let me think back on that. I've heard something about this mark on a wanted man, I think."

Longarm looked at the blue-traced pattern again. The mark was old but easily read. There was the outline of a skull and small lettering that read: Hoods Devils.

Longarm took a closer look at the pale, bewhiskered face of the dead man. Yeah, he thought, he was old enough to have been a cocky, shit-kicking kid when Hood's Texans were putting fear into blue-coated hearts. Longarm was almost positive he had once seen a Wanted flyer that mentioned such an identifying mark.

But he was also almost positive that it had been a very long time ago. He knew there was nothing in the current files about this man, or he would have remembered.

"Is your telegraph at the rail depot?" he asked.

"Ayuh," the town man said reluctantly. "Nobody there at this hour, though."

"Then, damn it, man, get the telegrapher up."

"You want 'im up, *you* get 'im up."

"Where is he?" Longarm asked with all the patience he could muster. It was not really a great amount of patience.

The town marshal gave Longarm an uneasy glance and got off his butt this time, leading the way out into the early morning sunlight without protest.

They got the telegraph operator out of his bed— and a fairly attractive young woman too, although

Longarm pretended not to notice that—and Wilbertson hurried away while Longarm shepherded the telegrapher to the depot and put the man to work.

While he was waiting for an answer to his telegraphed inquiry, Longarm walked over to the hotel for breakfast. It was still early, plenty early enough for him to have a jump on the holiday crowd, and he had the dining room nearly to himself. The only other people in the room were a couple—a graying, portly man and a very young and attractive woman—who looked like the only reason they were up at this hour was that they had not yet gotten around to retiring for the night.

Longarm ordered steak and eggs and a damned well immediate cup of strong coffee. He tried to get an eye-opener of rye too but was told no liquor would be served here on Sundays until noon. That did nothing to help his disposition.

He sipped at the coffee and did some thinking. He kept coming back to the same conclusion.

Someone had hired that arson job done.

And the arsonist was *not* the same man who had taken a shot at him the day before.

Whoever the rifleman had been, he was good with a rifle. Someone without experience would never have attempted so long a shot. And if he was foolish enough to try a shot like that, an amateur could not have come so very close to succeeding. It was only luck that kept Longarm alive that time. Luck and a dropped cigar.

He was going to have to remember that when he went wandering around Brownstone, Longarm reminded himself. Whoever had fired that first shot was still around and was very likely to try again.

And the arson attempt, that had to have been a

second attempt on his life, but by a second would-be murderer.

For sure, he thought, if the now-dead arsonist had been the same man who shot at him yesterday, the fellow would have been carrying a weapon with him when he came calling at the DeLucas' place with his can of coal oil and his blocks of matches. A hired rifleman was not likely to leave himself defenseless.

So the conclusion was inescapable. Two different men had been hired to kill him in two different ways.

The question now was whether both had been hired by the same unknown person, or whether the two had been acting independently of each other.

Interesting, he thought. Having one opponent who wished him dead was bad enough. The thought that there could be another was worse.

Longarm finished his meal and, feeling much better despite the lack of sleep, went back to the DeLuca house.

He felt awkward facing them again, feeling responsible for the harm that had come to them. There was no way his expense account would cover all the damages to their home, but he overpaid them for his lodging to a degree that would make Billy Vail groan when he saw the expense sheet, gathered up his things, and left.

"You are still welcome in our home, Marshal Long," the young Mrs. DeLuca protested.

But Longarm had to decline. "I can't help but feel that me being here last night might've had something to do with that fire, ma'am," he said. "I can't put your children in any more danger."

He said his goodbyes and accepted a grown-up

handshake from little Tony and hugs from the smaller kids.

The elder Mrs. DeLuca—he refused to think of her any longer as Grandma DeLuca but, damn it, he still did not know her right name—bid him farewell with a distant formality that belied the look of sorrow she had in her eyes.

That was fair enough, he thought. He was going to regret that particular parting too. But he did not want to endanger her any more than he did the kids.

He picked up his gear and carried it to the railroad station where the day clerk could look after it.

"No answer yet?" he asked the telegrapher.

"No, sir."

Longarm was not sure he could have remained as pleasant and polite about it if he had been rousted out of bed with a girl like he had seen earlier in the telegraph operator's room.

He left the depot and walked down toward the single livery in Brownstone, doing some thinking as he went.

Holiday visitors were already beginning to fill the street, and down toward the speaking platform vendors were setting up stalls to sell miniature flags and sandwiches and beer. The speeches would not begin again until noon, when church services would be ending, but already there were a few people drifting that way, and there was a busy, festive air throughout the town.

The remaining gunman, Longarm thought, was unlikely to make a try for him in a crowded public place. Which was a good enough reason to avoid crowded public places, damn it.

He was getting tired of waiting for someone else to make his moves and pick his times. Whoever the man was, he was still loose. Longarm wanted to correct that, and perhaps to have a word with the son of a bitch.

He went to the livery and found the hostler there. The man had been up long enough to have fed the horses waiting for hire and was engaged in cleaning out the narrow tie stalls when Longarm arrived.

"I want to hire a horse," Longarm said.

"Yessir. Single rig or a pair of fancies?"

"I don't want a driving rig. I need a saddle animal."

The hostler put his manure fork aside and pulled at his chin. "Don't have much call for them," he said. "But I got a couple light horses I think was broke to saddle once."

"Drag 'em out then."

Of the two horses the man brought out, only one looked like it had any possibilities whatsoever as a saddle horse. The other was a hairy, cobby old thing with cannon bones like tree trunks and a straight shoulder that would absolutely guarantee a trot that would loosen a man's teeth and give him a headache within half a mile.

"That one," Longarm said, pointing toward a stout but short-legged red dun that was eyeing the hostler with evil intent. Not a horse to turn one's back on, Longarm thought, but probably tough enough.

"Dollar an hour," the hostler said.

"Bullshit," Longarm told him. "Dollar a day, and I'll use my own saddle. You can save your gouging for the politicans wanting to take their girl friends for a Sunday drive."

The man grinned and shrugged. Apparently he was

not at all upset by the implied rebuke for his greed.

Longarm accepted the lead rope from the man and led the horse back to the railroad station.

The dun accepted the bit without a problem, but fidgeted when Longarm slapped the McClellan onto his back. It had probably been a long time since he had been in anything but harness.

The horse tried to sidestep away when Longarm went to mount. Longarm was not in a mood to take crap from the animal. He cheeked the horse and swung onto him before he was able to curve away the second time.

Longarm could not help but notice that the telegraph operator and the railroad clerk had both come out onto the station platform to watch the show.

Instead of bucking when Longarm gave him his head, the dun reared onto his hind legs, pawing at the air and coming dangerously close to overbalancing and falling over onto his back.

"The hell with you," Longarm muttered between clenched teeth. He came up in the stirrups and whacked the horse between the ears with a clubbed fist.

The dun came back down onto all fours, shook his head, and stood docilely waiting for instructions.

Longarm winked at the two disappointed men who were watching and took his time about pulling out a cheroot and lighting it.

He remembered that the Winchester had been messed with by a stranger during the night. He pulled it from its scabbard to reload and make sure the sights had not been knocked askew by the arsonist. He was pleased to note that when the rifle was drawn, the horse's ears came forward with interest. There was no sign of alarm from the animal. That was a good indication, he thought. If it came to that, he might be able to shoot off the animal's back, which was not something a man could safely do from just any horse.

Longarm nodded his satisfaction and laid the Winchester across the pommel of the saddle. If he needed the rifle he would need it in his hand, not in the scabbard.

"Good day, gentlemen," he said, and touched the spurs lightly to the dun's sides. The horse moved off at a smart jog, as if he had been a saddler all his life.

Longarm rode south, away from Brownstone and the quarry.

If the rifleman was watching and trying to follow, he was good. Longarm could see no one trailing behind, and there was no dust raised behind him.

He was offering himself as bait, and he was truly hoping that the son of a bitch would take him up on the offer.

There was a road of sorts that he could follow for the first mile and a half. It ended at a small and rather shabby dairy outfit that probably served the needs of Brownstone and nothing else. Beyond the dairy he cut across country and continued south.

Not too far, he thought. If the rifleman was following, it would not do for the man to become discouraged.

Longarm went another mile and found a place he liked.

A red sandstone outcropping stuck out of the hard soil like a ship's petrified sail, heeled over at an angle toward the mountains nearby. Off to the east there was nothing but rolling grass and abrupt mesas. To the south the land became wooded. Longarm wanted the rifleman, if he was going to come, to have to come to him across the grass that lay between him and Brownstone.

He rode the dun into the shade of the sandstone promontory and found a low-growing juniper to tie the horse to. If the animal was a puller, Longarm was going to have to walk back to town. But with all that buggy-driving experience behind him, the horse would probably stand forever once it was tied. He took the chance and left it there.

He walked around to the south end of the rock formation and climbed awkwardly, one hand occupied by the Winchester, to the top of the formation, about forty feet above the surrounding ground level.

The soft rock was deeply eroded and wind-carved near the top. Longarm had his choice of places to nest and took his time about picking one that would give him a good view along his back trail.

Then, satisfied, he tucked into a wind- or water-hollowed pocket where he could sit and wait without exposing himself to view from any direction but the west.

He made himself as comfortable as possible and settled in to wait.

Chapter 19

It was more than an hour before the rifleman showed up. Longarm did not mind. As soon as the man came into view, Longarm knew that the wait had been more than worthwhile. He sat and smiled and let the man come in closer.

He was afoot. That was the reason it had taken him so long to arrive. It was also, though, the reason he had raised no dust when he traveled and why Longarm had not been able to spot him trailing along behind.

The man was a tracker as well as a marksman. Longarm suspected he was as good at one as at the other.

He was also cautious.

Longarm's tracks disappeared from the grass around the west side of the rock formation. The rifleman chose to circle the formation on the east side. If the dun's trail led on to the south, he would be able to pick it up again at the other end of the formation.

But if the horse had been left behind the rock, if— as was indeed the case—an ambush had been laid for him, he did not want to follow the tracks blindly into the shelter of the red rock sail.

He was cautious and experienced. In a manner of speaking, Longarm admired that about him.

On the other hand, Longarm did not intend to give the man another opportunity to save the taxpayers the expense of a deputy marshal's salary.

There was already a stubby .44-40 cartridge in the chamber of Longarm's Winchester. Now he quietly eased the hammer of the gun back from the safe-cock detent and leveled the barrel down the sharp slope of the rock from his nest perched high on its top.

As the rifleman came directly below, Longarm leaned forward.

He let the man go another few paces, to make a return fire angle as difficult as possible. Then he called out to him.

"Whoa." He said it softly, without alarm or anger.

The rifleman stopped without protest. He stood motionless, not turning his head to look toward Longarm above and behind him.

"Think it over," Longarm said quietly. "You'll have a rough idea of where I am from the sound of my voice. You can try it if you like, of course. That's your choice. But I don't think I would, if I were you."

The set of the man's shoulders dropped slightly as the tension went out of him. He had made up his mind, Longarm thought. He was not going to try the brave but foolish thing.

The man let his rifle fall to the ground. They were

only about fifty feet apart. Longarm could easily see that the rifle was a superb example of its type, a heavy-barreled long Sharps fitted with Creedmore sights. Probably the caliber was as heavy as a buffalo rifle, but this particular weapon had been crafted with long-distance target shooting in mind. The stock carried a brass butt hook with an adjustable shoulder plate, and there was a palm-shaped rest attached to the ridiculously small forearm. It was damn sure only good fortune that had kept Longarm alive the one time this man had tried to shoot him.

"Can I turn now, suh?" the rifleman asked.

"Sure."

The man turned to his left even though a right turn would have been easier, considering their relative positions. Longarm was thinking about the rifle and did not notice immediately.

And then it was too late.

The rifleman dropped into a crouch as he completed his turn.

And during that brief instant when his right hand had been hidden from view, he had plucked a long-barreled target pistol from his waistband.

He was good. He was very nearly *too* good.

Longarm was not *exactly* where he had expected the marshal to be, but the gunman did not waste his single shot in a searching effort.

Instead he threw himself sideways from his crouch, spotting Longarm as he jumped and rolling on his shoulder to come up with the pistol aimed and ready.

It was with real regret that Longarm squeezed the trigger of the Winchester and sent a heavy slug angling downward into the man's upper body.

The fellow went down as if he had been poleaxed.

He lay face down in the dirt, and from his perch high on the rock Longarm could see a dark, spreading stain immediately over the man's spine in the small of his back. The bullet must have ripped through his gut to sever the spinal column as it exited.

With a wound like that the man would be dead within hours. If he was truly unlucky, though, he would live.

"Throw that pistol away," Longarm said over the sights of his Winchester.

There was no answer.

"Look, damn it, I know you can still move your arms. And I can see from here that you can't move or feel anything from your belly button down. Now throw that damn pistol away or I'll have to shoot you again."

He raised his head enough to look at the pistol for a moment, then tossed it aside.

Longarm let the hammer of the Winchester down to the safety position and climbed down the slope of rock. He squatted beside the dying man. "Do you want me to carry you around into the shade?" he asked.

"No, suh," the black man said. "Druther prop up heah where I can look out ovuh the plains." He smiled. "Awful good t' me, them plains was. Onliest place I evuh found where I was as good a man as any othuh."

"Abraham Issac Gort," the black man said. He gave Longarm a questioning look. "You did promise me, suh."

"I'll keep my promise," Longarm said. "I'll have the stone carved for you and see that it's set so it will last."

"Don' want none o' that red sand shit they take outa Brownstone, if'n it's all the same to you, suh," Abraham said.

"Granite," Longarm promised him. "Or marble, if I can find some."

Abraham nodded. He seemed satisfied by the assurances.

He was lying against Longarm's McClellan saddle at the base of the rock formation, propped up so he could see the grassland and the mesas stretching out for uncountable miles to the east. The red dun, unsaddled now and hobbled, was cropping grass nearby.

"Were you . . . ?" Longarm began.

"Naw," Abraham said. "The name, that's what you mean, right?"

Longarm nodded.

"Naw, that came later. Never had me a real name till Mistah Gort an' me got t' be partners. I thought it some fine favuh for him to let me carry his name as my own."

"Do you want to tell me about it?"

Abraham tried to shrug, but winced at the pain. "Not much to tell. Run away when I was little bitty. Off'n a place down in Texas. Al'ays loved to shoot, I did. Went up to Bozeman Trail, an' when I got me the chance I stole me a gun. Went to shootin' meat for the sojers. Buffalo. Lordy, there was a whole world o' buffalo then.

"Then most o' the forts up that way closed down. The wah back East an' the treaties an' such. Times got tough. Tha's when I met the senatuh. Course, he wasn't no senatuh then. He'd come up that way cowboyin', trailin' cows inta the minin' camps. But things was tough for him too. Got togethuh over a fire one

150

night. I'd used my last ca'tridge to take a buffalo, an' I was havin' myself a feast. He come along hungry.

"Turned out he had some ca'tridges would fit my old gun, but he wasn't no kind of a shot. We got to talkin' about that, an' I kinda showed off for him some. We got together after that. Go into some shit-hole of a town an' he'd make like he was drunk an' tell folks how this raggedy-assed nigger he knew was a better shot than the best they had. He'd work us up some bets, an' then I'd show 'em that his raggedy-assed nigger really *was* the better shot."

Abraham grinned and coughed a little. When he wiped his mouth afterward, there was a smear of red on the chocolate-colored back of his hand.

"Tha's how we got started," Abraham said. "Then we come down heah, an' the senatuh got respectable. Had us a pretty fair stake at the time, see, but the word was gettin' around. Wasn't so easy no more to sucker the bets. Always did love t' shoot, though." He shook his head. "The senatuh, he bought me that fine rifle over there. Give me all the shells I could want. Been goin' down in the quarry after workin' hours 'bout every day for years now. Shootin'. Sure have always loved that." He smiled, not at Longarm but at some distant memory.

"I'm glad you never got another crack at me," Longarm said.

This time the smile was directed at Longarm. "I am too, kinda. I never shot a man. Not colored, white, nor red. Didn' really want to nohow."

"I could try to get you back to Brownstone if you're feeling up to it," Longarm suggested.

Abraham smiled again. "Said I nevuh shot no man, suh. Didn' say I hadn't seen a good many as was shot.

151

You an' me both know I ain't gonna make it away from his spot right heah. An' it's a good enough place, I reckon. Good as any an' better'n most."

Longarm nodded. He had no argument to offer. "Why did Senator Gort want me killed?" he asked.

"Don' know that, suh."

"Would you tell me if you did?"

Abraham grinned. "Naw, but it happens that I don' know anyhow."

Longarm believed him. Not that it was really all that important. Longarm already knew all he had to about Gort. The rest would just be a matter of detail. There would be plenty of time for that.

"Could you do me one moah thing, suh?"

"What's that?"

"Take yo' saddle away an' ride off back t' town. I'm gonna try an' hold out till the sunset. I'd ruther not have anybody aroun' to hear me screamin' when it gets bad. You c'n send somebody out tomorrah to fetch me in for buryin'.."

Longarm thought about it, but only for a moment.

Hell, the man was not going anywhere. He was no danger to anyone. It seemed little enough to do for him.

"I won't forget the name for the stone, Abraham," he promised. "And maybe an inscription too. 'A good shot and a loyal friend.' Something like that."

Abraham smiled. "I'd like that real fine, suh. I truly would."

"All right." Longarm gathered up the fine rifle and the equally fine target pistol. Those, he thought, should be returned to Senator Gort. It was something he thought he should do himself, as a matter of fact.

He saddled the red dun, made sure Abraham was as comfortable as Longarm could make him, and rode north, back toward Brownstone.

Chapter 20

Despite the amount of time he had spent with Abraham, it was still only mid-afternoon when Longarm returned to Brownstone.

The street was nearly deserted, and down at the end of town the patriotic speeches were in full swing. The favored gentry had the comfort of chairs to sit in on the expanse in front of the platform, while the lower classes stood behind them or sprawled on the weedy gravel ground with their children crawling and bawling around them. Flags and red, white, and blue bunting were everywhere. It would have been a stirring and enjoyable sight if Longarm had not been preoccupied with other things.

He rode the dun to the edge of the crowd and stopped him there while he looked for the senator.

Another man, white-haired and heavy, his jowls bushy with snowy Burnside whiskers, was speaking at the moment. He was saying something about the greatness of this fair land and—undoubtedly in deference to the largely Italian population of Brownstone—was talking about assimilation and opportunity.

Gort was seated behind the man at the speaker's podium, the state senator's and gubernatorial candidate's chair squarely in the center of all the assembled dignitaries.

From the edge of the crowd some smart-ass kid who should have been old enough to know better lit a string of Chinese firecrackers and tossed them under the feet of the dun.

The crackers began to pop, but the little shit was disappointed in his hopes. The horse did not react beyond a brief flattening of his ears. He picked his feet up delicately and moved them away from the disturbance. Longarm gave the kid a look of hard warning and nudged the dun forward into and through the crowd.

Longarm rode the horse in front of the platform, directly in front of the man who was speaking. Longarm thought he had seen the man on the streets of Denver once or twice, but he did not know who he was.

The man looked puzzled at first and tried to lean around to address the crowd loudly past Longarm's intrusion.

He gave up when Longarm pulled his wallet out and showed his badge, first to the man on the platform and then out where the crowd could see.

"Deputy United States marshal," he declared in a loud voice. "Sorry to interrupt," he said, "but I'm here on official business."

The crowd and the men on the platform were silent

except for the sounds of a few crying babies out at the fringes of the gathering.

"Your business had best be highly official and highly important, Deputy, I warn you," the man who had been speaking blustered.

Longarm remembered who he was then. A congressman, no less, and as such plenty capable of causing trouble for Billy Vail and for one Custis Long.

"Yes, sir." Longarm touched the brim of his hat to the congressman and looked past him toward Gort. "But I believe, sir, you will agree that what I have to do now may save your party considerable embarrassment in the long run."

Actually, Longarm could not even remember what political party the congressman represented. He was only assuming that the man was a Democrat because of his presence here in Gort's home territory when Gort was to formally announce his candidacy for the governor's seat.

"Yes?"

Longarm reached down and untied the saddle strings that had been carrying the Sharps rifle on the left of his saddle. The Winchester was booted under his right leg.

He hefted the heavy Sharps and tossed first it and then the target pistol onto the platform.

Gort stood. It would have been impossible for him not to recognize the fancy weapons. And the meaning of their being now in Longarm's possession must have been quite clear.

"I am here," Longarm announced in a clear, carrying voice, "to place Senator Hiram Gort under arrest on charges of attempted murder and assault on a federal officer."

Longarm could not have gotten any more of a reaction if he had simultaneously dropped half a hundred
hornets' nests into the crowd.

People stood and gasped. Political hacks on the
platform around Gort leaped to their feet. Men shouted,
and more than a few idiot women started screaming.
Toward the back of the crowd, back where the working
stiffs watched, there were more than a few smiles.

Someone angrily grabbed at Longarm's bridle, and
some fool on the platform yanked a small-bore revolver out of his coat pocket and began waving it
about.

Son of a bitch, Longarm thought. *Who would have
thought that a little thing like an arrest would cause
this much commotion.*

Gort, meanwhile, was anxious to separate himself
from the crowd, and presumably from Deputy Marshal
Custis Long as well.

He threw a wad of papers he had been clutching
in his hand—his speech, probably—into the air and
turned to race toward the back of the platform.

The damned red dun, which had stood without
flinching when the kid threw the fireworks, blew up
when those papers flew into the air. He saw them and
went half crazy, trying to unload its rider and get the
hell away before something white and flimsy flew
over and bit him.

Longarm grabbed tight with his knees, clenched
his fist, and tried to repeat his earlier performance of
bashing the dun between the ears. His swing missed,
and the horse very nearly unseated him.

Gort dashed into the chest of the much larger man
who was still wildly waving the revolver. The senator
snarled at the idiot. They danced sideways for a long

157

moment, each trying to get out of the way of the other.

After a second or two of that, Gort tired of the game and punched the man in the stomach. When the fellow's hands came down, Gort grabbed the revolver away from him, shoved him bodily aside, and jumped off the back of the platform at a dead run.

Longarm, meanwhile, still had his hands full, between the plunging animal and the panicked crowd. People were stampeding out of the way of the rearing, bucking horse, falling over themselves and trampling one another underfoot as they tried to get away from the dun's hooves.

Some brave soul came running out of the crowd to make a grab for the reins. He got them in one hand, and Longarm decided to let him take care of the damned horse. He kicked his boots free of the stirrups and let the dun's next jump throw him clear of the saddle.

Longarm landed off balance and rolled with the direction of his fall. He dropped his shoulder and let the force of the fall carry him down and over and back onto his feet. He was running after Gort before he had time to come upright again.

Longarm dashed around to the back of the platform.

Gort was still in sight, running like mad for the road down into the quarry. That or the drop off the cliff was the only thing there was in that direction for him to run to.

Longarm slowed his pace to a trot and jogged patiently after the man. There was, he realized, no place for Gort to run to now.

State senator and would-be governor Hiram Gort crouched on the quarry floor, hiding behind a massive block of red stone that had been taken from the cliff face behind him but not yet cut into manageable slabs of rock veneer.

Beyond Gort, Longarm could see for the first time the artificial terracing of the scaffolds and ledges where the great blocks were being taken.

Above, at the upper edge of the manmade cliff face, he could see people lined up to stare down at the two men with the same fascination given to high-wire performers at a circus. Or, for that matter, to anyone who might be about to lose his life in public view.

Longarm ignored the audience and walked across the floor of the quarry pit toward Gort.

"Stop, damn you!" Gort shrieked.

Longarm could see the top of the senator's head but no more of the man. He continued to walk forward.

"I'm placing you under arrest, Senator. You might as well come quiet, because you're damn sure coming with me, one way or another."

"I have a gun," Gort warned. "I'll shoot if I have to."

"What good would that do, Senator?" He pointed toward the people who crowded the rim high above them. "There's a thousand witnesses up there. This time it isn't like that night when you killed your wife. This time the whole town is watching."

"I never killed Judith," Gort screamed. "I never. It was Abraham. He's the one. I should have killed that black bastard then. He's the one did it."

Longarm shook his head impatiently and continued walking toward Gort. "Abraham never killed anyone in his life, Senator. We both know that. And Abraham wouldn't have had a hundred dollars in gold to pay your arsonist pal." Longarm paused to light a cheroot. He continued to look across the stone block at Gort while he got it lit and flicked the match away.

"That one I couldn't figure out for a bit, Senator. But then I realized that it wasn't just me you wanted. You wanted to punish the DeLucas too because they were holding that meeting for me. Figured you'd put the fear into the peons, did you, Senator?" Longarm shook his head. "All this time, man, and you haven't yet figured out that you're dealing with a bunch of mighty good folks around here. You deserve to go to jail, you dumb bastard. Especially since I'd have gone away and not bothered you if you hadn't sicced Abraham and that arsonist on me. What happened then, anyway, Senator? Abraham turn you down on that one? Yeah, I'll bet that's it. He was a better man than you, Senator. It's a real pity he had to die because of you."

"I don't know what you mean about Johnson," Gort called. "I had nothing to do with that."

Longarm laughed. "Johnson, huh? Thanks. I couldn't remember his name. It will be waiting for me back at the telegraph office, I expect, but I hadn't remembered it." Longarm cocked his head and squinted against the smoke that was curling up around his face from the burning cheroot. "How'd you hook up with Johnson, Senator? Have something to do with his parole, did you? I'll check the records when I get back to Denver, of course, but I'll bet that's it."

Gort stood up from his concealment behind the stone block. He had a harried look about him. And he had the little revolver in his hand. The distance between the two men wasn't more than thirty yards.

Gort raised his hand and snapped three quick shots toward Longarm.

Longarm stood where he was, calmly smoking the cheroot. "Abraham said you couldn't shoot worth shit, Senator. Reckon I believe him about that too."

Gort fired again. The inaccurate little pistol barked twice and then snapped empty.

"Five is all you get with that kind, Senator."

Gort continued to cock and dry-fire the empty weapon.

Longarm tossed his cheroot aside and began to walk toward Gort again. He reached into a hip pocket and pulled out his handcuffs.

"No!" Gort screamed.

The dapper little senator turned and dashed to the back wall of the pit.

"No place to run to, Senator."

Gort climbed onto the scaffolding that rose high on the wall.

"No place up there, either, man," Longarm said. "It doesn't go all the way to the top. Even if it did, those constituents of yours up there wouldn't let you get away. You worked hard at being a son of a bitch, Senator. Now it's time to pay the piper."

Gort scrambled higher on the scaffolding, reached a platform, and dashed along it to climb the next section and then another. He was thirty feet up now and still climbing.

Longarm reached the bottom of the scaffold and put a boot on the lowest cross-member, testing it with his weight before he committed himself to it. It was beginning to look like he was going to have to go up after the silly bastard, cuff him, and haul him back down the hard way.

Gort reached a narrow ledge in the stone where a block had already been removed and lowered to the pit floor for cutting.

He jumped onto the ledge with a cry of glee and bent to pick something up. Then another.

Longarm could see what he held. They were sections of broken drill bit. Thick columns of tempered steel used to cut the initial holes for the quarrying process that still involved hammer and drill and chisel. Stonework had probably been much the same since ancient times when the Egyptians cut mammoth blocks of stone for their pyramids.

Gort reared back and threw the smaller piece of tool steel down at Longarm.

The steel hit the scaffold platform above Longarm and bounced harmlessly to the floor of the pit.

"I don't think that's going to do you a hell of a lot of good," Longarm said. He began to climb toward Gort.

The senator screamed something, raw sound rather than any intelligible words. He shuffled sideways along the ledge, trying to get a clear throw at the steadily climbing deputy.

From where he was, he could barely glimpse the lawman's sleeve as Longarm continued to climb patiently after him.

Gort shrieked again, his composure totally gone now, and took a step to the side to get a good throw down toward the deputy.

The ledge ended somewhat short of where Gort tried to step.

The little senator screamed again, but this time with terror.

He was off balance, and there was no longer anything to cling to, no scaffolding below him. Nothing but thin air and the distant floor of the quarry pit.

Longarm hung on to the scaffold supports and watched with interest as Gort plummeted past.

For such a small man, Gort made rather a lot of noise when he hit the stone floor. There was no more screaming after that.

Slowly and carefully Longarm began to climb down again.

He did not have to hurry.

Chapter 21

The opinion of the assembled dignitaries seemed to be unanimous. One and all, the gentlemen agreed that Deputy U. S. Marshal Custis Long should be drawn and quartered. Then fired from his job. The congressman who had been on the speaking platform earlier assured Longarm that his days of employment at the public trough were ended.

"Yes, sir," Longarm said politely as he elbowed past the man. "I'm sure they are, sir, but until someone makes it official, I have some work to do."

The congressman nearly had to break into an undignified trot to keep up with Longarm's swift stride.

"You have done enough damage around here, young man. I *insist* that you leave Brownstone immediately."

Longarm stopped. "Are you sure about that, sir?"

"Absolutely."

Longarm sighed and managed a long-faced look of great sadness. "As you say, sir."

The congressman, looking satisfied and self-important, turned and walked jauntily back toward his fellow politicians, most of whom were still in a state of shock after seeing the hope of their party first accused of a crime and then killed in a fall that all of them had to agree had been accidental.

Longarm walked away hiding a smile from the gentlemen. He saw no reason to ruin the congressman's satisfaction by telling the man that it had already been Longarm's intention to get the hell away from Brownstone just as quickly as he possibly could.

After all, Senator Hiram Gort, as it turned out, had had nothing to do with the assignment that brought Longarm here in the first place.

Adamo, the man Longarm had met at the DeLuca house, came toward Longarm leading the red dun horse. He handed over the reins and said, "I cannot thank you for the death of a man, Marshal, even though that death was not your fault. But in our hearts we know that now things may become better for us here."

"Or they may not," Longarm told him. "You get no guarantees in this country. Like those silly bastards was saying a while ago, it comes down to opportunities, not guarantees."

Adamo smiled. "We ask for no more than this."

Longarm started to lead the dun away, but Adamo stopped him.

"I almost forgot to tell you," he said. He smiled. "One of our people cleans the rail station, yes?"

"Yes?"

"She told me, a minute ago, no more, that one of the gentlemen of power has already sent a message to your boss asking that you be fired."

Longarm grinned. "Hell, Adamo, if Billy didn't get one of them once in a while, he'd think I wasn't doing my job."

Adamo had certainly been correct. By the time Longarm reached the depot, there was already an answering wire waiting for him there.

Not the response to his inquiry that morning about the arsonist named Johnson—which was a moot point anyway by now—but a message from Marshal Vail.

WHAT REASON BROWNSTONE QUERY WHY NO REPORT QUERY STAY THERE REPEAT STAY WHERE YOU ARE STOP AM TAKING NEXT TRAIN TO BROWNSTONE STOP EXPECT TO HAVE LONG TALK WHEN I ARRIVE VAIL

The telegraph operator looked rather satisfied when Longarm finished reading the message. But then, of course, he knew what was in it. Like the politicians in town, the man had little reason to like Custis Long today.

"When is the next train due in?" Longarm asked.

"Ask him." The man hooked a thumb toward the station clerk and added with a pleased smirk, "Schedules ain't my job." The smirk became broader. "Deputy."

"Thanks." Longarm asked the same question of the clerk.

"Next arrival's six-fifteen this evening. More or less."

"And the next departure?"

"Tomorrow morning, seven o'clock sharp."

"Thank you," Longarm said politely. He turned and

walked to the red dun tied nearby. Then, remembering, he returned to the clerk's station and retrieved the carpetbag he had left there earlier in the day. He carried it to the horse and tied it behind the cantle of the McClellan.

"Hey! Where do you think you're going?"

Longarm waved to the man but did not answer him. He mounted the dun and rode northeast toward Denver.

He had some checking up to do in the basement files of the federal building there, and on a Sunday night, and a holiday weekend to boot, he was likely to have a hell of a time getting into the building, much less getting into those files.

But he had to do it. It was necessary if he was going to be able to keep a date with an old acquaintance.

Chapter 22

Longarm tried to stifle a yawn, then said the hell with it and let it rip. He yawned hugely and stretched his sore, cramped muscles. If this bullshit kept on much longer, he thought, he was going to turn old before his time. Have to turn in a retirement notice before Billy could fire him. The prospect was sounding more attractive—even a firing instead of a retirement— with every passing minute.

For the second night in a row he had gotten almost no sleep. First there had been the hard run back to Denver. The dun, spooky as he was about papers flying through the air, was every bit as tough as he had looked. He made good speed and hardly raised a sweat on the twenty-odd-mile trip, much of which was taken at a swift canter.

Then he had had to find the custodian at the federal building—in itself no mean feat, as the man was known to imbibe from time to time and to be hard to wake during working hours—and bully his way into the records rooms.

The light there had been awful, the air musty, and the mass of records staggering. The custodian had not known any more about what was stored where than the resident mice did, so Longarm had had to do all the records digging on his own. When the records clerk came back to work on Tuesday morning, Longarm was certain to catch hell from that quarter.

But he still thought the effort was worth it.

Once he finally got done in the federal building he still had had to go to the Denver Police Department and shake the night duty captain out of his dreams so he could get into their records too.

All in all, he reflected, it had been a hell of a long haul. He doubted that he had gotten more than five hours of sleep, total, since he woke up Saturday morning. It was now just past dawn on Monday morning, and Longarm was feeling it.

Hell of a thing, he thought.

With the light getting stronger now, he shifted back another few feet so he could lean against the wall of the balcony he was "borrowing."

The dun horse, much better rested and better fed too than his temporary master, was tied around back of the building. To reach him if he needed the horse in a hurry, all Longarm would have to do would be to shinny down the drainpipe he had climbed to get up here, run back through the alley, and mount.

That might or might not become necessary. Whatever happened, though, Longarm intended to be prepared.

That old bastard was done pulling the wool over

people's eyes as far as Longarm was concerned.

The building he was watching was across the street from the balcony where Longarm was hidden.

It was a tall, narrow structure built of crudely milled lumber. Most of the other buildings around it were brick. Longarm guessed it had been here for a long time. The purchase—and thank goodness it had been bought and not rented those years ago, or he never would have been able to track its owner down from the city records—had probably been cheap.

More than likely the old place had paid for itself many times over by now.

There were no signs advertising the wares sold within, but the building was a place of business just the same. It was located square in the middle of Denver's tenderloin district, the old one near the stockyards, and had been a whorehouse for as long as any of the Denver police had been able to remember.

Quiet, they had said, and well run. No trouble there ever.

Considering past performances, Longarm found that to be interesting, and probably informative as well.

He had brought several box lunches to munch on and a canteen of water. He would have liked a cheroot too, but did not want to show any smoke. And a shot of rye right now would probably put him dead away for the next twelve hours. He settled for an apple and a ham and cheese sandwich for his breakfast.

A man with a delicate stomach, he reflected, could not make it in this business.

He finished the sandwich and tossed the wrapping paper back into the bag of food he had brought, then pulled out his Ingersoll and checked the time.

He had made a bet with himself. Just a gentlemanly little wager based on the way he would have handled things if he had been running the show. And if, that is, he was guessing correctly about what was going on this morning.

Seven forty-five. If he was right, it should not be long now. The night northbound from Trinidad, Pueblo, Colorado Springs, Palmer Lake, and Castle Rock had been due in at seven-thirty. Give a few minutes for late arrival, a couple more for unloading, more to find a hack. And then, what, ten minutes for the drive here?

He checked the watch again. Any time now.

A closed hansom, its plodding bay cob made almost presentable by the addition of a red, white, and blue plume on the bridle headband, turned the corner a block away and rolled toward the whorehouse.

Longarm grinned and told himself he had won his bet.

The noise of the cob's shoes on the brick street surface was loud. That and the grind of the hack's tire was about the only thing in the neighborhood to hear.

The cab pulled to a halt directly across the street from Longarm's balcony, and Pop Sweeley got out.

The old man was wearing a shabby but reasonably respectable suit instead of the prison garb Longarm had last seen on him.

Sweeley paid the driver with coins taken from his pocket and carefully sorted. He handed them to the driver and turned away. He had no luggage.

The driver of the hack sat on his box and counted the money he had been given. Then he turned and swore. Longarm could hear it clearly.

"Thanks a lot, y'old fart," he called after Sweeley.

Longarm grinned. No tip for that bucko this morning.

Sweeley ignored the driver and went up the steps to the front door of the whorehouse. The door was not locked. He opened it and went inside without knocking.

The cabby picked up his reins and drove away.

Longarm waited until the hack was out of sight before he climbed back down to street level.

He leaned against the wall of the building there for a few minutes to make sure there was no sign of movement at the curtains covering the windows of the whorehouse. Then he ambled across the street and up the same stairs Sweeley had just mounted.

Sweeley had not locked the door behind him. Longarm opened it and went inside.

There was no vestibule. The door opened direct into a large parlor. The place probably looked pretty good late at night, with the lamps glowing and with a few drinks inside the customers. With the morning light coming in through the cheap curtains, it just looked sleazy and in need of a thorough cleaning.

Longarm could hear voices coming from the back of the house. One voice he recognized as belonging to Pop Sweeley. The other was a woman. They sounded happy and excited. Longarm soft-footed across the worn carpet of the parlor toward the doorway that led into the back of the house. He leaned against the jamb and waited there.

". . . so glad," the woman was saying.

Sweeley laughed. "I told you I'd do 'er," he said.

"What about your friend down there?" the woman asked. "How much do we have to send him?"

Sweeley laughed again, louder this time, and longer. "That stupid sumbitch. He tried to hold me up for a bigger cut at the last minute. But the dumb bastard'd already give me my clothes and a good knife." He laughed some more. "Bastard won't have a chance to get any smarter. An' we don't have to worry about him peachin' on us neither."

"Pop! You didn't!"

"Course I did." Sweeley chuckled. "Leaves all the more for you an' me, baby."

That part of the conversation puzzled Longarm slightly. His memory and his intuition had brought him here because Sweeley's half-sister had been a Denver whore who was suspected of being part of the gang those years before. That had never been proven, though, and the woman had remained free. This house was in her name.

So why would Sweeley be calling his own sister "baby"? And why would a sister call him "Pop"?

Not that it mattered. The guesswork and the memory had brought him here. And here Sweeley was, right on schedule.

"You ain't moved none of it, have you, baby?"

"You told me not to, didn't you?"

"Good girl." Sweeley laughed and said, "Let's get it, kid, an' get the hell out of here."

There was the sound of a door opening, then footsteps receding on an inside staircase. It sounded like they were going down to the basement.

"What'll it be, kid?" Sweeley was asking the

woman. "Vancouver or maybe Bost..."

The voice became too faint for Longarm to hear any more.

He gave them another moment, then opened the door into the kitchen.

He heard a hissing sound from above and looked. A whore was leaning over the banister looking at him. She wore a flimsy robe that she had not bothered to belt closed. Without makeup, though, and in daylight, she offered no temptation for him to delay. She looked puzzled, obviously wondering what the hell he was doing there at this hour of the morning.

Longarm blew her a kiss, gave her a wink, and when into the kitchen. She could make up a story of her own to explain his presence. He did not want to be bothered at the moment.

The door to the basement stairs was ajar. From the top of the stairs Longarm could hear the sound of something grating, then something dropping onto the dirt floor, then some more grating. He folded his arms and gave Sweeley time to get to the hidden money from all those long-ago robberies and murders.

"Here, baby," Sweeley said with satisfaction.

Longarm stepped through the doorway and eased quietly down the stairs. The Colt was already in his hand.

Sweeley was crouched at the base of the back wall of the basement. He had a small pile of stone beside him, and there was a gap in the wall where the stones should have fit. Sweeley was busy pulling a tin box out of the hole. From the way he acted, Longarm guessed the box was heavy.

The woman who was with him was a surprise.

He had expected to see a used-up bawd of nearly

Sweeley's own age. Instead this was a young and attractive girl. She had pale red hair and a slim but nicely shaped figure.

He had seen her somewhere before. He had to search for it for a moment. Then it came to him. She and a tough-looking man had been on the same train south last week when he had gone to visit Sweeley. Of course.

He glanced behind him, wondering if the man she had been with then might still be around. He hoped not. It would be nicer if this all went smooth and easy.

But who the hell was she? he wondered.

Time enough to worry about that later. He eased down another step.

Then all hell broke loose.

Chapter 23

Behind him at the top of the stairs, Longarm heard an unmistakable, metallic sound that he knew altogether too well.

He spun, the Colt leading the way.

There at the top of the stairs in the open doorway was the plug-ugly the girl had been with on the train.

The fellow was wearing a dressing gown now and obviously belonged here. A bouncer, possibly, or a lover.

What the bastard was, though, was not important now. What drew Longarm's attention was the stubby outline of a .455 Webley revolver in the big man's hand.

The man fired before Longarm had time to bring his own muzzle to bear.

The large, slow-moving slug burned past Longarm's ribs.

The man groped awkwardly for the hammer of the Webley, but one chance was all he was going to get.

Longarm aimed his Colt from the hip and sent his first bullet into the big man's breastbone. The man took a half step backward, already reeling under the impact of the .44, and Longarm fired again.

The man was going down. Longarm's second shot caught him in the forehead and snapped his head back.

Longarm dropped into a sitting position on the basement stairs and swiveled toward Sweeley.

Or toward where Sweeley had been.

Aging or not, there was nothing slow and nothing soft about Pop Sweeley. He had a knife in his hand and was already at the foot of the stairs, swarming up toward Longarm with the knife held low and deadly.

An amateur will try to stab with an overhand motion. It is the man who holds a knife balanced lightly on his fingertips with the haft snug in the palm of his hand and the cutting edge upward that you have to watch out for.

Pop Sweeley knew what he was doing with cold steel, and he was intent on doing it to Custis Long.

He was already too close and too fast for Longarm to try to take him the way the book of regulations specified.

Longarm shoved the muzzle of the Thunderer in Pop Sweeley's direction and blew off the top of the old man's skull.

Even then he was already so close that his momentum carried him onto Longarm's ankles. And the thrust of the knife was so true that even after he was dead, Sweeley's weight drove the knife blade three-quarters of an inch deep into the planking of the staircase beside Longarm's leg.

Longarm looked first at Sweeley and then up toward the bouncer.

He did not hear any reinforcements charging to the rescue of the whorehouse inhabitants. But then, in a place like this that would have been unlikely anyway.

He got to his feet and was not particularly pleased to discover how shaky his legs had gotten in the last few seconds.

That was all it had taken, he realized. Little more than seconds. He shook his head and leaned on the stair railing to give his legs a chance to return to normal.

The girl was still down in the basement, standing beside the tin box that had to contain Sweeley's hidden loot.

Longarm did not feel up to walking down to her just yet, but his voice was steady enough when he asked, "How'd a pretty little ol' whore like you get hooked up with an old bastard like this? Or is the answer in that box, girlie?"

She gave him a proud, haughty look that he would not have expected to see in a place like this and stated, "I am no prostitute, sir. I am a property owner and a taxpayer and, sir, I am well aware of my rights."

Her head was held high, but tears were streaming down her face.

"And that old bastard, as you refer to him, was my . . . my fa-father." She broke down and began to bawl.

For the first time lately, Custis Long felt like something of an asshole.

Chapter 24

Billy Vail gave Longarm a look that was anything but reassuring. "Thought of any new and wonderful ways to screw up today?" he asked.

"Come on now, Billy. Damn it, I did what I had to do."

"Just by dumb, crazy luck, the way I see it."

"It worked out, didn't it?"

Grudgingly, Vail left his chair and poured a glass of Madeira for himself and a tot of Maryland rye for Longarm.

"Maybe," he admitted.

"Did you talk with the congressman this morning?" Longarm asked.

"Why do you think I'm in such a lousy mood this afternoon?"

Longarm grinned at him.

"The congressman is an eminently practical man,"

Vail went on. "I pointed out to the gentleman that it was much better for all concerned to have Senator Gort exposed *before* the official announcement of his candidacy than afterward. This way, no party candidate has gotten into hot water with the law. And no one can blame the party if a bad apple tries to run on their ticket but can't get onto it." Vail smiled. A little. "We don't have to mention things that might have happened but did not."

Longarm nodded and took a short swallow of the whiskey. It felt hot in his throat and warm in his belly. He enjoyed both feelings.

"I still don't know how you figured that Sweeley was trying to draw you away from Denver while he got up here and recovered his loot."

Longarm shrugged. "A little memory, a little hunch, a lot of hard thinking. Once I knew Gort hadn't had anything to do with him and I was on a wild goose chase there, I knew there had to be some reason for him to put me out there in Brownstone. I mean, he couldn't *count* on Gort getting pissed off enough to have me killed, though that would have pleased the old shit too. So I did some thinking on it.

"I know that holiday weekends are the busiest time for having visitors in at the prison. When there's the most strangers would seem the best time for a prisoner to try and slip out. And to have a definite timetable . . . well, that kind of implied he would have to have some help from someone at the prison. Which we found out by Sweeley's own admission. I thought about how I'd do it if I was him. And I thought about all that missing money that Sweeley had *not* paid to Gort, like he claimed, because Gort never had anything to do with him. Then I just worked it back from there."

"Why did he pick Gort to send you after?" Vail asked.

"That's one of the things I looked up in the records the other night. Until last year, Senator Gort was the legislative liaison with the Parole Commission. Apparently Sweeley tried to get his help once, and Gort ignored him. Pissed Sweeley off enough that when he needed a decoy to take me out of the picture, he used Gort for his make-believe target. He couldn't have known how well it worked. But then, everybody knew that Gort had come pretty much out of nowhere and had at least his share of political enemies." He shrugged. "Hell, it worked."

"So it did. Sort of." Billy sipped his wine and looked thoughtful. "There is one other small matter we need to discuss, Deputy Long."

"Yes?"

"I sent you a direct order by telegraph, Deputy. You were to be waiting for me in Brownstone when I arrived there on *that* wild goose chase. Not that there was no one there to meet me, of course. Half the damned state legislature was there with blood in their eyes, all of them screaming at me at the same time."

Longarm grinned at his boss.

"Why were you not there to meet me and take some of that heat yourself, Deputy?"

"Did you send me an order, Marshal? I can't say as I recall getting an order like that."

"The telegraph operator in Brownstone assured me you had read the message, Deputy. He even showed it to me. The wire was accurately transcribed. I checked that, you see."

Longarm grinned again. "See here, Billy, if that man had given me the message, why, he wouldn't have been able to show it to you afterward, now would he? So I just couldn't have got it."

Vail gave his best deputy a sour look. Then his expression softened and he shook his head. "You're a lucky son of a bitch, Longarm. I sometimes think you could fall off a moving train and land on your feet."

"Thinking of trains, Billy, I expect you'll be giving me time off now to take that train ride down to Manitou like you promised. I sure would like to go down and visit with Miss Morrisey for a few days."

Vail shook his head again. He tossed off the last of his wine and said with feigned weariness, "Get out of here, Deputy. And try to develop some respect for authority while you're gone. Will you do that for me? Will you?"

"Anything you say, Billy." Longarm stood. He drained his glass and set it carefully on the sideboard in Vail's office. He gave his boss a wink. "Anything you say."

Watch for

**LONGARM
ON THE GOODNIGHT TRAIL**

eighteenth novel in the bold
LONGARM series from Jove

coming in August!